A MATTER OF ETHICS

BY

PATRICIA ROBERTSON

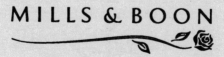

MILLS & BOON

*MILLS & BOON, the Rose Device and LOVE ON CALL
are trademarks of the publisher.
Harlequin Mills & Boon Limited,
Eton House, 18–24 Paradise Road, Richmond, Surrey TW9 1SR
This edition published by arrangement with
Harlequin Enterprises B.V.*

© Patricia Robertson 1995

ISBN 0 263 79362 1

*Set in 10½ on 12 pt Linotron Times
03-9510-49731*

*Typeset in Great Britain by CentraCet, Cambridge
Made and printed in Great Britain*

'Oh, I love it.'

Laura turned a shining face to Ben.

It was the first time she had looked at him with anything other than a distasteful expression. Even though her delight was not for him, his desire flared so strongly that he had pulled her into his arms before he could stop himself.

Still wrapped in the delight of being in this house again, Laura returned Ben's kiss.

His grip tightened as she kissed him as ardently as he was kissing her, but when his hand slipped under her tennis dress her head took over from her heart at last, and she wrenched away. '*No!*'

Patricia Robertson has nursed in hospitals, in district health, and abroad. Now retired, she is incorporating this past experience in her Love on Call medical romances. Widowed with two daughters, her hobbies are gardening, reading, and taking care of her Yorkshire Terries. She lives in Scotland.

CHAPTER ONE

'BEN KENDRICKS was telling me today that he gave up treating terminally ill cancer patients because he found it emotionally draining, and that he didn't regret giving up his consultancy in that field to take the senior surgical registrar's job here.' It came out in a rush as Sally Travers, Staff Nurse on Men's Surgical, put her tray of salad and yoghurt down on the staff canteen table, with a thump that rattled the cutlery, and sat down opposite her friend.

Laura put her knife and fork neatly together on her plate as she chewed the last mouthful. She took a drink of milk, then said, 'I don't care what he does or why.' She pushed her plate away. 'I just wish he'd stayed in London.'

It was true; she didn't care what Ben did or said, especially after the way he had treated her husband, but she wished she could stop the flare of desire just hearing his name roused in her. Every time since her husband had first introduced them, just after they were married, to see Ben or hear of him had affected her that way. That desire was mixed with loathing for herself, because the attraction had led her to many sleepless nights, for she had loved her husband and was distressed to find herself so attracted to another man—and that man David's friend.

When Sally had told her last week that Ben was to be the new senior surgical registrar at Ledborough

General Laura had been appalled, then relieved that she was a staff nurse in Accident and Emergency. At least she wouldn't see much of him there, and when he did come to examine a patient it would be Sister who would accompany him.

'I don't know why you don't make it up with Ben,' Sally said, as she piled her fork with salad and grimaced at the lettuce.

'Are you sure this dieting is helping?' asked Laura, really to divert her friend from Ben.

'Yes, of course,' Sally replied defensively. 'But no sidetracking.' She gave Laura a sharp look. 'It's two years since your husband died and too long to hold a grudge.'

'Grudge!' Laura frowned at her friend. 'He did nothing to persuade David to. . .' Tears crept into her hazel eyes and she had to pause a moment. 'To have chemotherapy for his terminal cancer. I know that his type of cancer couldn't be cured, but having chemotherapy would have given him a few more years. I found that out after David had died, from one of the other doctors.'

'You didn't tell me that,' Sally said, her fork in mid-air. 'Why didn't you complain to the hospital?'

'David's last wish was that I would not blame Ben.' She sighed. 'He must have known. I had to respect his wishes.'

She remembered as if it were yesterday Ben, who had been David's consultant in the oncology unit at a London hospital, telling her harshly, 'There's nothing I can do. You'll just have to accept that David is going to die.' It was written in her heart. And not only that, but also the loathing for herself as she had felt desire clutching her as she had looked at Ben when he'd told her. But how could she tell her friend that?

Sally reached forward and took Laura's hand. 'I'm sorry,' she said remorsefully. 'Forgive me.'

She looked so stricken that Laura laughed. 'Of course I do. What would I have done without you? You took me into your flat after my father's firm transferred him to Canada and my parents left, and put up with all my self-pity and moans about Ben being the executor of David's will.'

That still rankled. David had been fifteen years older than Laura, and rather old-fashioned in his ways. He had told her that Ben was to be executor of his will and she had been annoyed at this and dismayed, but David had already been ill when he had mentioned it and she had not wanted to quarrel with him.

When he died she'd found that he had tied up his will, so that she could not spend the considerable amount of money he had from his grandfather without consulting Ben. It was only after the will had been read that she'd understood why David had said, 'I've made sure that no one will take advantage of you when I die. It isn't that I don't trust you, but there are so many men about who would take advantage of your money.'

She had been too distressed at the thought of his approaching death and trying to hide her distress from him to query what he had meant.

If only he had not put her in the charge of his best friend, she thought for the thousandth time.

Laura's face softened when she remembered how

protective David had been of her. It had been one of the things she had liked about him when they were courting, but she was not to know that after their marriage her independent spirit would rebel. She had spent many a day biting her bottom lip so as not to quarrel with him.

It had been hard for Laura not to be angry with David when he wouldn't discuss his illness with her. 'I don't want you to be touched by any of this,' he had said, and had smiled so charmingly that her anger had left her. It had been so like him to consider others.

But she was not going to sit back like an obedient child. She had caught up with Ben as he was leaving the unit after she had been visiting David and had said, 'Chemotherapy. What about that?'

He had turned a stony face towards her and said, 'Chemotherpay will not save your husband.' And had walked quickly away.

'But it may give him a few more years,' she had shouted after him.

He had stopped, but not come back, just said distinctly, with his back towards her, 'You're a doctor, are you?' Then turned and quickened his stride.

Sally was still looking guilty, so Laura said, 'If I had a sister I would want her to be you.'

This compliment brightened Sally. 'Thanks.'

They left together.

'I'll cook the meal tonight,' promised Sally as she waited for the lift to take her to Men's Surgical.

'As long as it's not something from your diet,' Laura said drily over her shoulder as she walked on.

*   *   *

In Accident and Emergency, Laura was treating a patient with the curtain drawn back when Ben Kendricks cast a shadow over them. He was tall, dark and handsome, brown-eyed and intelligent; everything a girl could ask for in a man. Laura's nursing friends enthused over him constantly, but if she never saw him or heard from him again it would make her happy.

'Sister about, Staff?' Ben asked.

Laura looked up at him with an expressionless face. 'Sister Jackson's in the office,' she told him curtly.

'Well, that's where you're wrong. I looked there and she isn't.' His tone was sharp with the anger her cold dislike roused in him.

As he looked at the face turned up to his he wondered how she had fallen in love with David Osbourne, who was studious, quiet and gentle. Quite unlike the vibrant Laura. Perhaps it had been David's serenity that had attracted her, as it had himself.

Laura was not a particularly beautiful woman, for her hazel eyes were too far apart and her mouth too big in a smallish face, but there was an arresting quality about her. Her light brown hair had been curly when he had first met her, but now it was shoulder-length and wavy.

It was not her face that made men turn to look at her twice. The first time it was to look at her figure, which was perfect, and the second was to feel again the aura of sexuality she possessed.

Ben had been on a lecture tour with his chief in America when David had phoned him. 'I'm married to a wonderful girl. It would have been too long to wait for your return to be best man.' His voice had been full of happiness. 'I met her three weeks ago and it was love at first sight.'

'You're sure you know what you're doing?' Ben had asked, then had thought how silly the question was. David would never do anything without careful thought.

'Absolutely. You'll love her,' he said enthusiastically.

On Ben's return, David had introduced him to Laura, and the attraction between them had been so strong that Ben worried David would see it, and kept away as much as possible from the couple.

Then David had been diagnosed with cancer. Ben had been his consultant, and when David had died he'd left him with a burden he had no way of lifting.

'Well, if you look again, I'm sure she'll be in the office now,' Laura snapped, bending her head to hide the blush her awareness of him had roused.

Even though the day was over halfway through, and he had been in Theatre this morning with a heavy list, he was looking more attractive than ever, particularly smart in a dark grey pin-striped suit with a maroon tie that made his white shirt appear even whiter.

Just one glance at him etched every detail of his appearance into her memory. His brown eyes, clear and alert, his skin, fair for a dark-haired man, his almost black hair, with just a strand or two of silver.

Laura knew why he had come. A young derelict with suspected appendicitis had just been brought in.

'Thanks,' Ben replied sarcastically, and turned away.

She couldn't stop herself listening to his footsteps as they receded, and she had to concentrate hard on what she was doing to blot them out. 'I'll try not to hurt you, Mrs Day.' Laura smiled reassuringly at the middle-aged, fair-haired woman with the swollen wrist that she was attending to.

Gently she slipped Margaret Day's hand through the circular frame with the tubigrip on it until it reached her elbow and then withdrew it, leaving the tubigrip in place. When the frame reached Margaret's fingers, Laura pushed it back along the way it had come, so that a double tubigrip was now stretching from fingertip to elbow. She then took a pair of scissors and, lifting the area over the thumb, she cut a piece away to allow the thumb to slip through.

'Is that more comfortable?' she asked with a smile.

'Oh, much better thank you, Staff,' Margaret said. 'I'm just glad it wasn't broken, as I'm going on holiday tomorrow.' The worry lines on her face had receded. 'Stupid of me to stand on the windowseat to draw the curtains. Fancy forgetting that it curved and stepping on the bit that wasn't there.' She laughed.

'The doctor said you won't need a sling, but keep your hand tucked into your coat and raise it on a pillow when you're sitting down,' Laura told her. 'You'll probably find that the swelling will go down quite soon, and then you won't need the support.' Laura helped Margaret put on her jacket. 'Go to a doctor if you're worried,' she advised as she ushered Margaret out.

Laura was just clearing away when Nurse Pearson came to her and said, 'Sister would like you to go with Mr Kendricks to see a patient.'

'Very well,' Laura said, inwardly groaning.

She made her way to the end cubicle where the patient, a teenager, dressed in jeans and a dirty T-shirt, lay on his side with his knees drawn up. He didn't have a jacket and his trainers were dirty and worn. Laura could see a hole in the bottom of the left one. He should have had his shoes removed, thought Laura, frowning in annoyance. She would have to speak to Michelle Pearson. He didn't even have a blanket over him.

Laura's frown aggravated Ben. 'Sorry to drag you away, Staff,' he said, his voice thick with sarcasm.

'You didn't, Mr Kendricks,' she said, with indifference.

He glared at her and she at him, but a groan from the patient drew their attention. This was not the place to be thinking of themselves. In this they were in agreement, though unaware of each other's thoughts.

They turned to the patient. Ben handed Laura the notes. She opened them and found that their patient, Robert Wilson, was aged nineteen, of no fixed abode, and had refused to give his parents' address.

Laura sighed. Another who was homeless, she thought, glancing at the pale, pinched face with compassion. There were quite a few teenagers like Robert, begging on the streets of Ledborough. What was his problem? she wondered as she moved to the head of the bed on the opposite side to Ben.

'Turn on to your back, Robert,' she said gently, and as she assisted him to do so a small gasp escaped her lips. The young man had a look of David. His face was the same shape, a thinker's face, his hair the same colour, blond, and his eyes the same blue.

'Staff.' Ben's sharp voice brought her head up quickly, and she looked at him with sad eyes, but she was not seeing him; she was seeing David as he had lain dying.

Then her glazed eyes cleared and she did see Ben, but seeing him brought back fiercely what she thought of his betrayal of her husband as a doctor.

'Help me to examine the patient, please,' Ben said curtly. He knew what she was thinking.

The patient's need of her brushed her anger aside. She smiled down at Robert and said, 'I'm just going to undo the button of your jeans. The doctor wants to examine your stomach.'

The young man's face was flushed, and he moved restlessly. 'I'll do it,' he said.

He had no particular accent, and Laura wondered what a boy like this, probably from a well-off home, with a private school education, was doing on the streets as she lifted his T-shirt up a bit for Ben to palpate Robert's abdomen.

Ben's hands were the strong hands of the surgeon. Laura found herself watching his fingers as they gently touched the patient, and desire to have those hands touch her filled her with a sudden longing—a longing she found distasteful. How could she want this man?'

Since her husband's death she had found her work especially satisfying, particularly in this department, which was very varied. One minute comforting a patient's relatives, the next calming a child, then dressing wounds, applying slings, taking bloods. Severe accident cases roused the adrenaline, and working as part of a team gave her enough stimulation.

Her social life consisted of hospital parties, going to the cinema with girlfriends and chatting with the hospital staff at the local pub.

She had plenty of opportunity to go out with men, and had done so in the company of others, but she had not encouraged any of them. They had not roused a spark in her. It was only Ben who did that.

Laura heard Ben ask, 'Did the pain start here?' as he felt Robert's umbilical area.

Laura straightened her back and looked down at Robert.

'Yes,' Robert said, looking up at the big doctor anxiously.

Ben's fingers dipped into the area of the right iliac fossa, and when he lifted them away sharply Robert gasped.

'That hurts,' he said, giving Ben a reproachful look.

'Sorry.' Ben's eyes were sympathetic. 'Have you been sick?' he asked, as Laura helped Robert adjust his trousers but did not fasten them.

'Yes, and my mouth's very dry.'

'Pop out your tongue.'

Robert did so. It was furred, and his breath smelt unpleasant.

Ben reached for the notes to check the temperature. It was not recorded. 'Would you take Robert's temperature, please?' he asked Laura sharply, raising an eyebrow.

'Yes,' she replied in some confusion, and as she did so she reminded herself to add this to the complaints she would have for Nurse Pearson.

Laura recorded the temperature and pulse—both were raised—and showed the recordings to Ben.

'I don't think we'll disturb him further to do a rectal examination,' he said quietly, for only her to hear. 'It's definitely an appendicitis and we had better operate immediately.

He turned back to the patient. 'You have an inflamed appendix,' Ben explained, 'which will need to come out right away.' He glanced at the notes to check that Robert was of an age to consent to the operation. He was; he was nineteen. 'Have you had anything to eat or drink lately?'

'No.' A spasm of pain crossed Robert's face. 'I felt too sick.'

'Is there anyone you would like us to contact?' Ben's eyes were compassionate, and Laura had to steel herself against his kindness. She did not want to like him.

'No.' The answer was abrupt and defiant.

'You'll have to sign the consent for operation form,' Ben told him.

'I understand.'

'I'll be back in a moment,' Laura promised, and went with Ben to the office.

Sister looked up from a pile of paperwork. 'Shall I phone Theatre?' she asked.

Celia Jackson was just forty-five. The staff had held a party for her two days ago on her birthday. Her fair, wavy short hair was tinted, her round face pleasant, and her figure generous. The white trousers and tunic top, made of a material that repelled fluids and worn by the sisters as opposed to the staff, whose uniform was pale purple of the same material, did not flatter her short figure, but she was popular and an experienced nurse.

'Please,' Ben said, with a smile that curved his lips. Kissable lips. Involuntarily the thought leapt into Laura's head and horrified her.

'Staff, tell the patient that he'll be going straight to Theatre. They'll prep him there, but get a specimen of urine and test it before he goes, please.' She paused for a moment, her kind face looking troubled. 'I have a son that age. I hope he doesn't leave home like Robert!' It was almost as if she was thinking aloud.

'No fear of that with a mother like you,' Ben said from the door, with a big smile on his face.

'Away with you,' Celia said, laughing.

If only Laura could forgive Ben for not encouraging her husband to have chemotherapy. If only she could forgive herself for the attraction she felt for Ben, Laura thought as she made her way back to the cubicle. If only she could rid herself of the hard core of misery that had afflicted her so often since David's death.

In the cubicle, Laura asked, 'Is there anything I can do for you?' her heart filling with compassion when she saw the drawn face. She smiled gently down at him as she brought a dampened cloth to bathe his face.

'I just couldn't cope with university,' Robert blurted out. 'And I knew my parents wouldn't forgive me for dropping out.'

'Are you sure?' Laura asked in a concerned voice.

Robert sighed. 'Yes.' His expression was as cynical as his tone, and it saddened Laura. She had been happy at his age.

'I knew medicine wasn't what I wanted after the first three months and tried to tell my father, but he wouldn't even listen.' Robert frowned with pain and groaned.

'Don't think about it now,' Laura said gently. She had brought a urinal, explained what it was for and left him for a moment to use it.

The porter brought the trolley and Laura helped transfer Robert to it.

'I'll come and see you,' she promised.

'Would you?' he asked, looking vulnerable.

'Of course.'

She went and tested the urine and told Sister that it was normal.

She almost forgot to see Nurse Pearson. Normally she was efficient, but her attraction to Ben had disrupted her. It was catching a glimpse of the nurse that reminded her.

'Nurse Pearson,' she said as she reached Michelle, who was hurrying away from a cubicle with an uncovered bedpan. 'If Sister catches you, she'll throw you out of Casualty,' Laura told her. 'Where's the cover for this bedpan?'

Michelle Pearson blushed. She was pretty, fair-skinned, erratic, but kind and caring. She was always wearing earrings, which she was told to remove every time, and her make-up was far too thick. Something else she was being told off about frequently. Michelle was the original dizzy blonde. 'I—I——' Tears filled the blue eyes. 'I don't know.'

There seemed to be more than lack of thought in Michelle's reply. The girl was upset, but it did not seem related to the telling-off she was about to receive.

'Let's go and empty this,' Laura said kindly.

In the sluice, Michelle was about to put the bedpan into the disposable unit when Laura stopped her. 'Is the urine required for testing?' she asked.

'Oh, yes.' Tears ran down the nurse's face. 'Oh, I'm so sorry.'

Laura took the bedpan from her and poured the contents into a specimen glass, then put the bedpan into the disposable unit and switched it on. 'Do you know the patient's name?' she asked, as she washed her hands and indicated that Michelle should do so too.

'Yes. It's Sonia Pearson, my mother,' Michelle rushed to say. 'She was knocked down in the street by a man running for a bus and fell on her side. Russell thinks she's fractured a couple of ribs and may have bruised her kidney as she fell on to her shopping-bag full of tins of dog food.'

Laura put her arm about Michelle. 'Did you tell Sister the patient is your mother?'

'No.' Michelle looked at Laura, tears wet on her face. 'I only just found out when I was told to take the bedpan away and test the urine.'

'We'll test the urine now,' Laura said. 'And then tell Sister.'

The test showed blood in the urine. 'Is that bad?' Michelle asked anxiously.

'Not necessarily,' Laura tried to reassure her as she washed her hands. 'Come on. Let's go back to your mother,' she said gently.

Dr Martin Russell was the duty houseman. He was a broad-shouldered young man of medium height. His dark brown hair flopped on to his forehead, giving him a little-boy look. Laura had seen patients glance at him doubtfully. It was obvious that they thought him too young, but he was competent, and older than he looked—twenty-seven—but the inference made him inclined to be mildly aggressive.

'Thought you were never coming,' he said crossly. 'Where's the other nurse? At least she was competent.' He threw the notes he was writing up down on to the bed. Then he saw Laura and his face cleared.

Before he could speak, Laura said, 'Mrs Pearson is Nurse Pearson's mother.' Her tone was cold. She did not approve of doctors speaking to nurses like that in front of a patient. If they thought a nurse incompetent they should tell Sister. It was her job to reprimand the staff.

'Oh.' Martin glanced from mother to daughter, unable to hide the surprise in his eyes.

Sonia Pearson was not at all like her daughter. She was dark-haired, sallow-skinned, plain of face and large of build. The complete opposite to Michelle.

'I'm all right, darling,' Sonia said, trying to hide the pain that speaking was causing her.

'Oh, Mum,' wailed Michelle.

'You stay with your mother,' Laura told her, before she turned to Martin. 'I'll just let Sister know about this and then I'll help you,' she said, handing him a piece of paper on which she had recorded the urine test result.

'Very well,' Martin said in a chastened voice.

When Laura returned she said to Michelle, 'Sister says you can go off duty now, Nurse Pearson.'

'Thank you.' Michelle's gratitude made her blue eyes seem larger.

'Thanks for the help, Laura,' Martin said as he watched the trolley, with Michelle holding her mother's hand, making its way to X-Ray.

Laura knew he was attracted to her. He had asked her out on a couple of occasions, but she had refused.

'Think nothing of it,' she replied coolly.

The rest of the day passed without any major accidents being brought in. The usual—cuts, broken ankles, eye injuries—and various other casualties were treated in their order of importance.

Laura was glad when it was time to go off duty. She felt drained—not by her work, but by the effort needed to forget her attraction to Ben.

If she had known that a further blow was to await her when she arrived at the flat, she might not have been so eager to go home.

CHAPTER TWO

'HI,' CALLED Laura as she closed the front door after her.

She hung her jacket up in the hall. Turning to see why Sally had not answered her, she found both Sally and Geoffrey, Sally's boyfriend, standing together in the lounge doorway, holding hands, with big grins on their faces.

'Congratulate us,' Sally said, her brown eyes smiling. 'We've just become engaged.'

Laura rushed and hugged them both. 'I'm so happy for you,' she said.

Geoffrey Young was the solicitor who had handled Sally's affairs after her mother died. They had met again six months ago at a friend's party and the attraction they both felt at the time of her mother's death—but had not allowed to flower because Geoffrey was married—had flared between them again. He was divorced now, and there were no children to consider.

Geoffrey was ten years older than Sally. He was the same height as she was, five feet nine, but slimly built and balding at the front.

'Come and have a glass of champagne,' Sally said, pulling her friend into the lounge where Geoffrey was already pouring the sparkling liquid into champagne-glasses.

Laura accepted a glass from him and said. 'Here's

to you both. May you have a long and happy married life.'

And, as she said those words, she was surprised and pleased to find that she did not feel a tug of grief. Perhaps she was putting David's death behind her. They had only been married a year when he was diagnosed with cancer, but that year had enriched her life. The only thing that had marred it was the attraction that had flared between them when Ben came to dinner.

'So when's the wedding to be?' she asked as they sat down.

'As soon as possible,' Sally told her, her hand in Geoffrey's as she sat beside him on the couch.

'I want to be a bridesmaid,' Laura demanded, with laughter in her voice.

'Of course,' Sally said happily. 'It's only going to be a quiet wedding, at a registry office.' Then her face became serious and she looked unsure of herself. 'We're going to live in Geoffrey's flat, which means that I'll have to sell this one,' she finished in a rush.

'Of course you must,' said Laura quickly, to reassure her friend. 'I'll find another place.'

'What about buying the flat?' Sally suggested, her eyes brightening.

Laura thought for moment. 'I suppose I could ask Ben.' She sounded doubtful.

'I'll ask him to my birthday party tomorrow,' Sally said, not mentioning that she had already done so without consulting her friend. She thought the party would be a good opportunity for Laura to meet Ben socially. It might improve relations between them.

'We thought we'd announce our engagement then,' she continued. 'A drink or two might make Ben more amenable.' Her voice was filled with enthusiasm. 'It will give him a chance to have a look around the flat as well.'

'Oh, I don't know about that,' Laura said quickly, as a vision of his face smiling at Sister flashed before her eyes and she felt, again, the pull of his sexuality. 'No, definitely not,' she added vehemently.

'Oh, well.' Sally hid her dismay at hearing this. She would just have to try and put Ben off.

'I'll phone Ben about the flat,' Laura said. It was something she dreaded doing, and usually she spoke to him through the solicitor, but. . .

'OK.'

Laura did not notice the guilty expression on her friend's face; she was too busy trying to blot Ben's features from her mind.

In bed that night, Laura found she could not sleep. Her life was changing, and perhaps it was time it did so.

She had been in a rut since her husband's death and had been too lethargic to do anything about it. Her work filled her days and sporting activities most of her off duty.

Her main friend was Sally, and the announcement of her engagement jolted Laura and made her realise how dependent she had become on her friend.

Laura turned her pillow over. She was twenty-six. Was she going to live in the shadow of her husband's death for the rest of her life? David would not have wanted her to. He would have wanted her to live a full life.

Right! Well, that was what she would do. The pain of his death had dulled to a bearable ache. She would start her new life by asking Ben for the money to buy this flat tomorrow. She loved the large rooms, and began to feel excited at the thought of how she would transform them to suit her tastes.

Turning her pillow over again, she lay down and fell immediately asleep.

But the next day, Saturday, she was kept busy preparing for the party, and when she did take a moment to phone the number Ben had given her there was no reply.

When she mentioned this to her friend, Sally said, 'I think he was going to Birmingham today, to attend a lecture on keyhole surgery given by a surgeon from the States.'

'Oh, well, I'll just have to try and get hold of him tomorrow,' Laura said, and continued to fill the vol-au-vent cases with a chicken and mushroom mixture, unaware of the apprehension in her friend's eyes. Sally had not been able to contact Ben either, to put him off coming to the party.

The rest of the day was spent by the girls in washing extra glasses, plates, cutlery, cups and saucers. They arranged everything on the large sideboard in the lounge. It was to be a buffet meal.

Geoffrey came at lunchtime, with boxes of beer and bottles of wine. 'Where shall I put these?' he asked as he put the last box down in the hall.

'I think the kitchen,' Sally decided.

Laura came in just as Geoffrey was kissing Sally. She had seen them kiss many a time, and it had not bothered her, but today her heart suddenly beat faster, and it wasn't because she wished she were being kissed by Geoffrey. It was because, suddenly, she wished she were being kissed by Ben. She blamed working with him so closely in Casualty for this, and not the fact that she couldn't banish him from her thoughts.

'Look what Geoffrey gave me for my birthday,' Sally said, holding out her wrist, on which gold charms swung on a gold bracelet. 'I've always wanted one of these.'

'It's lovely,' Laura said, bending her head to hide the blush thoughts of Ben's lips on hers had roused, and to examine the different charms.

'Now, where shall I put out the booze?' Geoffrey asked, his eyes alight with happiness.

'I'll show you,' Sally said, taking him into the lounge where a table had been set aside for the drinks.

The party was due to start at eight o'clock. At seven o'clock, Laura had had her shower and was in her bedroom, staring at her clothes hanging in the wardrobe.

She seemed to be seeing things with new eyes. Were these dreary clothes really hers? They were dark in colour, mainly black, grey, navy and beige. Mourning colours, she thought. Even their style was old-fashioned. She must look at least ten years older in them, if not more.

Next week she would give them to Oxfam and buy some new ones. Sally had been asking her to do this for ages, but Laura had not bothered. What should she wear this evening that would not make her look as if she was attending a funeral?

There was a suitcase on top of the wardrobe which had been there since she had moved in. Perhaps there was something in there that would not be so dull.

Laura stood on a chair and pulled it down. It came with a rush and fell on top of her, showering her with dust. Picking herself and the suitcase up, she placed it on the bed. It was not locked. Opening it, she found inside her wedding-dress. She had forgotten it was in there.

Laura lifted the delicate, embroidered ivory dress from the case. The material was still crisp. Sadness touched her, but did not linger.

As she laid the wedding-dress aside, and looked once more in the case, she found another dress lying there. It was green, the colour of the green in her hazel eyes.

She had always associated green with bad luck, since she had fallen into a boating lake as a child, wearing a green dress. But she had not been able to resist the dress when she was buying her trousseau, because it had made her look so attractive. Superstitiously, though, she had not worn it on her honeymoon, in case it did bring bad luck.

Now she drew it from the case and shook out the folds. The soft material of the skirt fell into place as if it had not lain in a suitcase for three years. She held it up to her face and saw how it drew the green from her eyes. David had never even seen the dress, so it didn't remind her of him, but would it fit?

Laura put it over her head. It was stupid to be superstitious. Not wearing it had not saved David. The material caressed her skin as it slipped over her, and seemed to bring her body to life, just as a man's hand—Ben's hand?—smoothing her flesh might do. It was a troubled face that looked back at her from the mirror. The dress fitted perfectly.

Then her chin firmed. What was she making such a fuss about? She had not betrayed her husband with Ben while he was alive. These feelings that Ben roused just meant that she was a woman whose celibacy since her husband's death was ended. It was time for her to take up her life again, and that meant in the true sense—love, maybe marriage.

The dress made her look more than attractive, it accentuated her curves. She gave her reflection a pleased smile before she slipped on the matching shoes that she had found in the case.

'My, you look gorgeous,' Sally told her when Laura found her in the kitchen, a bright red-flowered apron covering Sally's black chiffon blouse teamed with a black, straight skirt. She put down the plate of crisps she was holding. 'When did you buy that?'

'Some time ago. I forgot I had it.'

'What a change from those greys and blacks.' Sally surveyed her friend with admiration.

'Yes, isn't it?' Laura agreed. 'I'm intending to buy new clothes.'

Sally gave her friend a hug. 'About time too.' Should she tell Laura that Ben was coming? Perhaps he wouldn't. He might not get back in time. She would leave it and hope for the best.

'Is there anything I can do?' offered Laura.

'Yes, take these crisps into the lounge.'

'Right.'

Laura was just putting the plate down when the bell rang. 'I'll get it,' Sally called. 'It'll be Geoffrey.'

It was, and soon afterwards colleagues from the hospital and friends of Geoffrey's started to arrive.

Laura was passing the crisps and nuts among the guests when Martin slipped his arm round her waist. 'You look gorgeous,' he said admiringly as he pulled her closer.

Laura's resolve to restart her life did not include Martin, who managed to be almost everywhere she went—even to joining the same sports club. It aggravated her. She had never given him any encouragement.

Pushing him none too gently away, she said, 'Mustn't touch.'

'Waiting for Ben Kendricks to arrive, like all the others?' he asked in a mocking tone.

What you think doesn't bother me, Laura thought, and was about to move away when she realised what he had said. 'Ben Kendricks?'

'Yes, Mr Benjamin Kendricks, the senior registrar on Sally's ward,' he said sarcastically.

Sally knew she didn't want to see Ben, Laura thought. Surely she hadn't invited him? Anyway, she was not going to let Martin see what a shock his news had given her, so she just shrugged.

'So you're like all the others, attracted to the handsome registrar.' He could not keep the envy from his voice.

Suddenly Laura realised that he had taken her shrug to mean that she *was* eagerly awaiting Ben's arrival. Here was a chance to prick Martin's infatuation for her. She was not going to lie, but her expression gave the impression that Martin was right.

Laura saw that she had succeeded when he became crestfallen. She should have felt guilty, but she didn't. Perhaps he'd stop pestering her now.

She went to look for Sally and, seeing that her friend was not in the lounge, went into the hall, meaning to look in the kitchen.

The bell rang and Sally flew out of the kitchen to answer it. She opened the door to Ben. 'I——'

Before she could continue, Ben, looking past her, made Sally swing round. The guilt on her face showed Laura that Ben was expected.

'I. . .' Sally blushed. 'I. . .' She didn't know what to say, and was astonished when Laura smiled at Ben. As astonished as he was. Sally's mouth gaped.

Ben was holding out a parcel to Sally, but his admiring eyes were still on Laura.

'Thanks,' said Sally, taking the gift and unwrapping it. It was a black china cat with an expressive face. 'Oh,' Sally gasped with pleasure, and flung her arms round Ben's neck. 'How did you know I love cats?'

Ben pulled his eyes away from the attractive Laura reluctantly. 'I have my spies,' he said with a smile.

As soon as Laura had seen him all that telling herself that these feelings of desire he roused were just due to her setting aside her grief and taking up her life again flew away, as gossamer in the wind. She'd been lying to herself.

That attractive smile dried her mouth, even as she realised that she had never known Sally liked cats.

She did remember, now, Sally saying jokingly that

a cat would add the finishing touch to their single status, but she had not realised it had been a hint and had vetoed the suggestion, not liking cats herself. It was further proof of her friend's consideration for her. Had she really been so wrapped up in herself? she wondered guiltily.

Sally was pulling Ben towards the lounge. 'It will have pride of place on the mantelpiece,' she said. 'And you deserve a drink.' She glanced at Laura. 'You'll get him one, won't you, Laura?'

Martin was looking towards them, so Laura smiled at Ben and said, 'Yes,' in an eager way.

Ben went with her to the table of drinks, somewhat astonished by this softening in Laura.

The room was so crowded that Laura could feel his breath on her neck as he followed her. It warmed her skin and heat swept through her body.

Quickly she slipped behind the table, putting it between them. Her confusion made her say, 'What would you like?' even though she knew he drank whisky.

He gave her a slow smile. 'Whisky, please. Have you forgotten?'

'It's been a long time,' she said briskly.

'Yes, it has.' There was note of sadness in his tone. The last time had been at David's funeral.

His expression was reflected in her eyes as she passed him the drink. David's death bound them together still. She filled a glass of white wine for herself and took a gulp.

Now would be a good time, before he started to circulate, to ask him about buying the flat, she decided.

She linked her arm in his to prevent him moving away and Ben was further amazed.

How stupid of her to do that, she thought, feeling a shiver of desire catch hold of her at his nearness. She was going to pull away when she saw Martin was still looking in their direction. 'Come over to the windowseat,' she said, giving Ben a smile that was really for Martin's benefit.

'Leading me astray?' Ben joked, giving her that gorgeous smile that seemed to be melting her.

She wanted to reply, tartly, that a man of his experience would never be led astray, but she didn't want to alienate him, so she said, 'But of course,' in a jesting way.

He laughed, pleased at this change in her attitude towards him.

'I know how busy you are so I want to take this opportunity to ask if I might buy this flat. Sally's moving to Geoffrey's house now that they're engaged.'

The relaxed lines on his face tightened. 'I see.' He bent to take a big drink of whisky to hide the bleakness in his eyes. When he looked at her again it was gone, and his expression was impersonal. He took another sip. 'I don't see any problem, if the price is satisfactory.'

It was the first time he had agreed to a request from her without an argument, and it astonished Laura so much that she was speechless.

She drank some of her wine to account for the pause and then said, 'Have I proved myself a responsible citizen, as you have no objections?' she asked as he rose.

'You were always that,' he told her quietly. 'You just needed someone to help you following David's death.'

He glanced at her dress and saw the change in her. The sadness had left her. She looked more like the old, vibrant Laura. He guessed that she had thrown off her grief and decided to start life afresh.

'David's instructions were that once you had recovered from your grief, and shown that you could handle your money wisely, my executorship could be terminated,' he told her quietly, then added, 'It was left to my discretion.'

'Oh, was it?' she said angrily. 'Twenty-six is quite old to be told that I am now an adult.'

'A reply like that makes me think that I've made a mistake,' Ben said, his eyes amused.

Laura blushed. He was right. 'Sorry,' she said stiffly.

'Forgiven. I'll make an appointment with the lawyers that will suit us both.'

'Right.'

As Laura stayed where she was, and watched his tall, straight-backed figure join a group of nurses from his ward, she suddenly felt insecure.

Ben had been a strong figure in the background since David's death. She had been so busy despising him that she had not realised how much she had relied on him, until now, when his support was to be removed.

CHAPTER THREE

THE party finished at about one o'clock, but it was past two before they went to bed.

'I'm sorry about not telling you I'd already invited Ben. I wasn't able to contact him to put him off, either,' Sally said guiltily. 'And I thought perhaps he mightn't come.'

'That's all right.' Laura smiled at her friend.

'What did Ben say about your buying the flat?' asked Sallly as they had a cup of tea after tidying up.

'He said it would be OK, providing the price was right,' Laura told her as she stirred her tea. 'He also said he was going to let me manage my own affairs now.'

'My, that's an improvement.' Sally's surprise was evident in her expression. 'That should please you. It will mean that you won't have to have any contact with Ben, apart from professionally.' She smiled at her friend.

'Yes.' Laura tried to look pleased, and hoped that her friend would put the dullness in her voice down to the lateness of the hour.

Sally pushed back her chair. 'Well, I'm for bed,' she said as she rinsed out her mug. 'It was a good party.' She looked down at her black chiffon blouse, Laura's present. 'Thanks again for the blouse. It was admired by everyone.'

'Glad you liked it,' Laura said, rising to join her

friend at the sink to wash her mug. Sally had wanted the blouse for some time, but had not been able to afford it.

Laura slept badly that night, her dreams nightmarish. She had slipped off a ledge, and was holding on to it by her fingers. Ben reached down and caught hold of her wrist, but it started to slip from his grasp. She woke bathed in perspiration.

Sunday was a sunny, blue-skyed day. Laura spent it trying to push Ben from her thoughts. In the afternoon she went to the sports centre, hoping a game of tennis would distract her from him.

She was just glancing about for a partner when Ben came in. 'Looking for someone to play with?' he asked, with a twinkle in his eye at the double meaning.

'Tennis—yes,' Laura said coolly, as the same meaning struck her.

She wished she had only answered in the affirmative when he asked, 'What else did you think I was willing to play?' The amusement was still in his eyes.

'Nothing with you,' she said, more tartly than she had meant to, because his masculine figure in white shorts and tennis shirt was rousing thoughts she would rather not have. He was extremely attractive—more than attractive, sexually magnetic.

Ben had been admiring her slim form, her brown legs and smart white sleeveless tennis dress that showed her brown arms.

Laura, seeing this, wished she had worn shorts, knowing that the frilly white pants that went with the dress might remind Ben of the time David and she had played in a foursome with Ben and a partner.

Perhaps he wouldn't remember how he had commented on a similar outfit. 'Makes you look like a child,' he had said, his eyes laughing.

It had annoyed her at the time, because it had been true, but David had put his arms round her and given her a squeeze. 'An adorable child,' he had said, smiling at her with love. The memory caught at her for a moment, but did not upset her.

'Wearing frillies again?' Ben asked deliberately.

Damn, he'd remembered. 'None of your business,' she said, looking around for someone else to give her a game.

Ben was also looking, but no one came into the clubhouse. 'Do you think you could manage to have a game of tennis with me without scowling all the way through it?' he asked drily. 'There doesn't seem to be anyone else.'

It was either that or go home, and Laura did not want to do that. She needed to tire herself out so that she would sleep better, but his words had made her feel uncomfortable. He sounded as if he thought she was being childish, so she said, 'OK. And I'll try not to scowl.'

He laughed and nodded.

The sun was shining as she walked beside him to the grass court, casting shadow reflections of the net on to the court. Endeavouring to apply herself to the game, and not to notice Ben's fluid movements, needed all the concentration in her power.

Every time he reached for a ball his athletic frame stretched, showing the perfection of his body which his tennis outfit could not hide, causing her game to be erratic.

'You need practice,' he said as they finished with him the winner. 'You used to play well.'

Still do, she felt like saying, when I'm not distracted. 'I'll bear your advice in mind,' she said wryly.

'I don't suppose you'll come for a drink with me?' he asked in a resigned way.

Laura would have loved a drink, but just the nearness of him walking beside her past the other courts made her feel hot with longing, so she said, 'Er—no.'

Ben was not to have his drink, though, for they had just reached the last of the hard courts when an alarmed cry of, 'Don't try it, darling,' turned their heads in the direction of the voice.

A well-built man of about forty had not taken the advice of his female partner and was jumping over the net. He cleared it with his front foot, but his back foot caught the net and he fell heavily forward on to his right side, hitting his head, shoulder and side on the hard surface of the court.

Laura and Ben rushed forward. The lady who had cried out was kneeling beside the still figure. She looked up as Laura reached her first. 'Henry would do it,' Eve Hall said, with tears in her eyes. Laura knew her by sight from the club.

Ben explained who he was, and bent to examine the unconscious form. 'Looks as if he has a fractured humerus.' He indicated the top part of the man's arm, so that Eve would know what he was referring to. 'Probably bruising to his ribs and maybe a fractured skull.' The bright day allowed Ben to see that Henry's pupils were uneven and his level of unconsciousness was deeper than Ben liked. 'Send for an ambulance, will you, please, Laura?' he asked, glancing up at her.

She nodded and hurried away, returning with a rug the receptionist had found in the lost property box.

'His unconsciousness seems to be lifting a little,' Ben reassured the white-faced Eve as Laura covered Henry with the rug.

'You wouldn't think my husband could hurt himself so badly, would you?' Eve asked, her eyes anxious.

'It's because he's a heavy man,' Ben explained.

The ambulance arrived soon afterwards. The paramedics recognised Ben, who explained what he suspected Henry's injuries were.

Ben and Laura went with Eve to the ambulance. 'Thanks very much,' she said, tears of gratitude filling her eyes.

'Glad we could help,' Ben said, patting her shoulder.

Just his coupling them by the word 'we', drew Laura closer to Ben, as if she had no power to prevent herself. I must fight this, she told herself.

As she made to turn away, Ben asked, 'Could you give me a lift home?'

So he wasn't staying for a drink. Laura couldn't very well refuse him. She didn't want to alienate him so that he would change his mind about giving her control of David's estate.

'Where do you live?' she asked as he climbed into

her old Metro. He was really too big for it and made the car seem small.

'Rosemary Gardens,' he said. 'Know where it is?'

'You forget, I was born in Ledborough,' she said as she turned into Thornton Road.

'No, I hadn't forgotten,' he said quietly. Laura had been married in Ledborough.

It had been a mistake to offer him a lift. Sitting so close to him in the confines of the car made her breathless with desire. She only hoped he would not suspect.

'You don't need to hold the wheel so tightly. It won't fly away,' he told her wryly.

She glanced sideways at him and saw the grin on his face, she also saw the desire flare in his eyes as they met her own. 'I always hold the wheel tightly,' she informed him haughtily.

His laugh showed that he didn't believe her. 'Turn left at the next corner,' he instructed.

'I know,' she answered sharply. Nervousness at his nearness caused her to take the corner too quickly, so that the wheel hit the kerb. This is the last time I'm giving him a lift, she told herself.

As Laura drove along Rosemary Gardens she envied him living there. It was a street that had always attracted her ever since she had been taken to a party as a child to the house at number ten.

Trees lined the street, outside old houses with bay windows. She remembered the coolness of the hall, the size of the rooms, and especially the dark blue wallpaper covered with flowers. It had reminded her of pictures she had seen, of Victorian children living in such a house.

She could not believe it when Ben asked her to stop outside number ten. She turned an excited face to his. 'Does the lounge still have that blue paper?'

'Yes.' He looked surprised.

'Can I see it?'

'Of course,' he said.

Seeing his puzzled expression as they left the car and went up the path through the small garden, she said, 'I've always loved this house, since I came here as a child to a party.'

'Ah!'

'Have you bought the house?' she asked.

'No. It's just rented, with an option to buy,' he told her as he turned the key in the blue door and ushered her into the hall. It was as cool as she remembered. A staircase curved up the side with a banister, the polished wood shining in the darkened hall.

Without waiting to ask, she went into the lounge. It was as she remembered it, even down to the mahogany furniture. 'Oh, I love it.' The words escaped involuntarily as she turned a shining face to his.

It was the first time she had looked at him with anything other than a distasteful expression. Even though her delight was not for him, his desire flared so strongly that he had pulled her into his arms before he could stop himself.

Still wrapped in the delight of being in this house again, Laura returned his kiss. Then, when the kiss started to deepen and she realised what she was doing and who it was that was kissing her, she found she was unable to pull away. All the suppressed feeling of the last three years had sprung into life, and she was revelling in the sensations Ben's kiss was rousing. Never had she felt before such excitement and passion as now swept over her.

His grip tightened as she kissed him as ardently as he was kissing her, but when his hand slipped under her tennis dress her head took over from her heart at last, and she wrenched away. '*No!*' she cried, trying to still the trembling of her body.

Even as she cried out, Laura could not quell the want in her as she saw the unquenched desire darkening Ben's eyes, and his face still soft with aroused passion.

Laura longed to throw herself back into his arms, and fled from the house to stop herself from doing so. She had to wait in the car for a moment or two, so that her trembling body could settle.

'I hate him, I hate him,' she said out loud, her voice sharp with vehemence, feeling she had betrayed her dead husband by letting Ben kiss her. Ben who had betrayed David.

But as she drove home she could still feel the pressure of his lips upon hers, the smoothness of his hand upon her flesh, and her longing nearly drove her insane, so that she had to stop the car again to stem her trembling and fight to recover herself. No one had ever affected her this way.

David's love had held a gentle passion to which she had responded in a similar manner. She had not been aware that she was capable of being roused to such a pitch of excitement so quickly. To what heights of passion might she and Ben have climbed? she wondered as she parked the car.

A sadness came over her as she entered the flat, a sadness for herself. Ben was a man, she admitted, who could rouse her beyond herself. But a man she could not have.

CHAPTER FOUR

BEN phoned Laura on Monday just as she was about to leave for work, to suggest a suitable time to meet at the lawyers. 'Will Friday be all right?' he asked.

'Only if it's before three. I'm on duty then,' she told him.

'I'll arrange it and let you know the time,' he said, and rang off.

Had he been affected by the kiss? she wondered, as she fought to control her pulse, that the sound of his voice had started racing. Then she remembered the dark passion in his eyes. He was as drawn to her as she was to him; she knew that. The physical attraction that had been felt between them when they had first met was there, only stronger now.

Laura pushed these thoughts aside as she entered A and E. She changed into her uniform and listened with the rest of the staff to the report.

A woman pushing a baby in a well-worn pram entered the department at the same time as Laura left the office. She had short, spiky hair dyed red, and was wearing tight black jeans, a white T-shirt with the picture of a pop group printed upon it and a black leather jacket. She looked very young, with a heart-shaped face, and wore three earrings in her earlobes but no make-up.

Seeing the nurse's uniform, she caught hold of

Laura's arm. 'There's something wrong with my baby,' she said in a belligerent way.

Laura saw that the baby, who was about six months old, was limp and had the dull eyes of an old person. She had seen it before in a battered baby and said calmly, 'I'll get the doctor to look at your baby immediately. What's your name?'

'Rose Powell, and this——' she looked down at the baby '—is Timmy.'

Laura put her into the first cubicle and went to find sister.

Sister Jackson came out of the end cubicle at that moment, with Ben. Bother, why did he have to be here? Laura thought irrationally as her heart fluttered.

Their heads turned as Laura approached. 'Yes, Staff?' Celia Jackson asked.

'I've just put a mother and baby into the first cubicle. I think the baby might have been battered,' she told them in low voice.

'Would you like me to have a look at the baby?' Ben asked Celia.

'Please,' she said. 'John's out on an emergency call with Medic One.' Celia gave him a grateful look. 'It would be better if Staff goes with you as the mother has already met her. We don't want to startle her.'

The young woman looked up at Ben as they entered the cubicle. 'I'm Dr Kendricks,' he said. 'I've come to have a look at your baby, Mrs Powell.'

Rose paused for a moment, and in that moment Laura thought she saw apprehension in the mother's eyes, and wondered if Ben had noticed.

Rose lifted the baby out of the pram. It whimpered as she touched it. Ben took the child from her. For a man who had no children of his own he handled the baby with confidence, and a gentleness that touched Laura. He must be fond of children, she thought, seeing how his face had softened as he gently laid Timmy on the bed.

He did not ask Laura to undress the baby, but did it himself. The child lay with its limbs lying limply on the bed. Timmy started to whimper again, and this affected Laura so much that she wanted to snatch him up and cuddle him, and tears gathered in her eyes.

Ben glanced up at her at that moment, to where she stood at the head of the bed, and his eyes softened. She was such a caring person.

It was a warm day, but the child had been dressed in an anorak and trousers. Laura realised that the pinkness of his face was due to the amount of clothing he had on and not to good health, for gradually his face paled as he cooled.

Ben examined the naked child. It took all of Laura's willpower to prevent herself from crying out. The small, rather thin body was bruised. Every time Ben touched him with gentle fingers, Timmy whimpered.

Rose was on her feet at the end of the bed. 'He fell off the couch,' she said, and to Laura her tone was too matter-of-fact. It was as if she was telling them a book had fallen.

'Fell?' Ben's tone was cool.

'Yes,' Rose said defiantly.

Ben looked at the heart-shaped face raised to his. 'We'll have him X-rayed,' he said evenly.

How can he be so calm? wondered Laura, unable to look at the mother because she knew her eyes would show how angry she was. How could any mother let her child be so battered? Then an even more awful thought struck her. Perhaps the mother was the one who had caused the injuries.

'Staff!' The sharpness of Ben's tone made Laura jump. She pulled herself together and hoped her face didn't show her thoughts.

'Fetch a blanket. No point in re-dressing the child,' he said.

Laura was glad to leave. There were some baby blankets in the linen cupboard. She drew one out and returned to the cubicle.

Gently Laura wrapped the baby in the blanket. Rose made no move to touch her son. Her face was stiff, with what Laura thought was dislike.

Ben was writing in the case-notes and filling in the X-ray form. 'We'll have to admit your son, Mrs Powell. I'll tell Sister that you're staying with the baby.' He handed Laura the X-ray form.

'Miss Powell,' the young woman said defensively. 'And I won't be staying.'

So the mother must have been the one who had battered her son, thought Laura as she gently carried the whimpering child to X-ray.

Medic One arrived back with John and the paramedics. Laura could hear the monitor bleeping as they passed her. Another cardiac arrest, she thought.

'Mr Kendricks phoned,' the radiologist said when

she arrived in X-ray. 'He wants me to phone the results through to the ward. You're to take the baby there when he's X-rayed.'

Laura nodded, and waited until Timmy had been X-rayed, then she took him to the children's ward. She was surprised to see Rose Powell in the waiting-room as she passed the door. Laura had thought the mother would have left.

Sister Beatrice Nicholson, Bea for short, was in the office. Ben was there as well, waiting for the X-ray results.

Bea rose. 'I'll show you where his cot is,' she said, gently touching the child's face. Timmy was crying piteously.

Bea was only five foot two, and with such a young-looking face that she could have been mistaken for one of the children except for her uniform. She did not have a chip on her shoulder about it, though, unlike Martin.

The children's ward was bright and airy. Disney pictures were painted on the windows, and scenes on the walls. The general atmosphere was cheerful.

Laura laid the baby down in the cot Bea indicated. 'The mother doesn't want to see him,' she whispered as she covered the whimpering child.

'Will the police be informed?' Laura asked, looking down with compassion at the baby.

'It will depend on what the paediatrician thinks,' Bea said, rather stiffly, Laura thought. Bea beckoned to a nurse. 'Sit with Timmy, please, Nurse Roberts,' explaining that the baby had fallen.

Laura returned to the office with Sister. She wanted to hear what the X-ray results were.

Bea raised an enquiring eyebrow as she looked at Ben, who was just replacing the receiver. 'Timmy has a hair-line fracture of his skull, but apart from that just bruising.'

'Do you think he did fall off the couch?' Bea asked.

How can she be so calm? thought Laura, bursting with anger on Timmy's behalf.

'It's possible,' Ben said with equal calmness. 'I'm sure Joe Carter——' Laura knew him to be the paediatric registrar '—will think he should be kept in for twenty-four hours for observation. Then he can be reviewed.' He rose to his feet. 'I'll speak to Joe,' he promised.

Laura could not understand what to her seemed lack of concern, and her expression showed it.

'Thanks,' Bea said, and turned to Laura. 'Was there something else?' she asked.

Laura heard the coolness in her voice. I wonder why she doesn't like me? she thought.

Ben had risen to his feet. 'Perhaps it would be a good idea if Staff questioned Miss Powell,' he said. 'She was the first one to see her.'

Laura didn't want to do this. She didn't feel impersonal enough. That was one of her failings. She became too involved.

'Yes,' Bea said. 'She might learn something.'

Laura did not like the way Bea was speaking about her, as if she was not there, nor could she ask what Bea meant. Her brows drew together in a frown.

'You'll find Miss Powell in the waiting-room, if she hasn't gone,' Bea said.

'Very well, Sister,' Laura said stiffly, giving Ben an angry look, and turning so quickly that she didn't see the thoughtful expression on his face.

Rose Powell looked up as Laura entered the waiting-room. Her eyes narrowed, and there was a hardness about them that immediately tightened Laura's face. She was about to close the door when Ben appeared. Now what does he want? She wondered, trying to quell the sudden rush of desire that rose at the sight of him.

'Miss Powell,' he said, sitting beside the slim woman. 'Your son has a hair-line fracture of his skull.' His eyes were sympathetic. 'We shall be keeping him in to observe him.'

'I don't care what you do with him,' Rose said belligerently. 'He's just a nuisance, and his crying drives me mad. That's how——' She stopped suddenly and shrugged.

So she *was* responsible for the baby's injuries, thought Laura, her expression hardening.

'Did you let the baby fall?' Ben asked quietly.

Why is he being so gentle? Laura wondered, thinking of poor little Timmy's pathetic face.

Again Rose shrugged. 'Think what you like,' she said impudently. 'You can't prove it.' She jumped to her feet. 'I'm off.' And she slipped quickly from the room before Laura could stop her.

'Well!' Laura's mouth gaped. 'You'll inform the police?'

'No,' he said quietly. 'The——'

Laura interrupted him. 'No?' Laura had to fight hard not to roar at him.

'No,' Ben repeated quietly.

Laura was furious, and part of her anger was because she had responded to his kiss. How could she have forgotten that he had betrayed David? How could she have given in to the attraction she felt for Ben? Disgusted with herself, she lashed out at him with words. 'Like David.' Her tone was sarcastic.

Ben stepped backwards as if she had hit him. His face became like stone. 'Things are not always what they seem,' he said, so stiffly that the words were clipped.

'Well, they seem pretty clear to me,' Laura said angrily. 'David's life could have been extended by the use of chemotherapy if you'd pressed him harder, and Timmy could be protected against further damage by being taken into care.'

'You know what your trouble is?' Ben said, his face reddening with anger and frustration at not being able to tell her about David. How he cursed the Hippocratic oath he had taken when he became a doctor, the oath that made a patient's confidences sacred. 'You're inclined to make snap judgements.'

Laura was horrified to feel excited by the passion of his anger. It made her speechless for a moment. Then her own anger rose higher. 'I consider that unfair. You know nothing about me.'

'I know enough,' he said, quietly this time, and it was his quietness that made her wonder what he meant. But he was gone before she could ask him.

Enough? What did he mean? Well, she wouldn't think about that now. She must return to Accident and Emergency.

The rest of the day was spent in treating mostly

minor injuries. At four o'clock, Laura was attending
to a patient complaining of earache. 'Did your own
doctor see you?' she asked.

'I don't live in Ledborough,' Colin Bradley, a red-
headed thirty-year-old dressed in a grey suit, told
her irritably. 'I'm at a computer conference here. I
know I should have gone to my own doctor before I
left, but I thought it would settle.'

Laura was annoyed with herself. Obviously she
hadn't been concentrating when she read the notes
or she would have seen that the patient was a
temporary resident. Irrationally, she blamed Ben for
this. He'd been at the back of her mind all day.

Laura lifted the auroscope and looked gently into
Colin Bradley's left ear; pus obscured her seeing the
eardrum. She examined Colin's face more carefully.
He looked more unwell than just an ear infection
should make him and he seemed drowsy. 'I'll just
take your temperature and then get a doctor to see
you,' she said.

'I was hoping to go home today,' Colin said,
looking anxious. 'My wife's pregnant and due to
have the baby next week.'

Laura smiled reassuringly, more reassuringly than
she felt. She popped the thermometer into his mouth
and took his pulse. It was not unduly raised, but his
temperature, when Laura removed the thermometer, was exceptionally high. This man needed
immediate treatment. 'Do you have a headache?'
she asked.

'Yes.' He drew his eyebrows together. 'And the
light hurts my eyes a bit.'

'Have you been sick?' she asked.

'No, but I feel it,' he replied.

They were not in a cubicle, but in the room set aside for the treatment of minor cases. 'I'll take you to one of the cubicles,' she said soothingly. 'It will be easier for the doctor to examine you there.'

In the cubicle, she helped him climb on to the bed. 'That feels better,' Colin said as he lay down, and closed his eyes with a sigh.

Martin was just passing as Laura left the cubicle. 'Could you see this patient right now?' she asked, catching hold of his arm.

'I was just going for a cup of tea,' Martin complained.

'This man needs to see someone right away,' Laura said firmly. 'He has an ear infection and is complaining of headache and——' She was just going to add photophobia and nausea, when Martin interrupted her.

'Oh, all right.' Impatiently he pulled back the curtain and entered the cubicle. 'How long have you had this trouble with your ear?' he asked Colin in a sharp way as Laura sat Colin forward.

'Three days,' Colin told him.

After a cursory examination, Martin said, 'You should have seen your GP.' His tone was curt. 'We have far more important patients to attend to than people with an ear infection. It is an emergency unit, you know.' He picked up the notes. 'We'll give you an antibiotic and I'll write a letter to your own doctor. Go and see him when you get home.'

Laura was appalled, but managed to hide it. 'I'll be back in a moment,' she told Colin, following Martin out of the cubicle.

In the office, she said, 'Don't you think he should be admitted?' her face showing her concern.

'I didn't know you were a doctor,' he said sarcastically.

'But the light hurts his eyes and he feels sick,' she insisted.

Martin tutted. 'Photophobia you mean, don't you?' His tone was even more sarcastic.

'Yes,' she said impatiently. 'So?'

'So what? The light hurts my eyes on a bright day like today, and he's probably had too much beer with his meal.' He bent his head to write again in the notes.

'Light hurts whose eyes?' Ben had entered without them hearing him.

'A patient in cubicle two,' Laura said quickly, aware of Martin's scowl.

'He's got an ear infection, that's all,' Martin said dismissively.

'Did he tell you that the light hurt his eyes?' Ben asked, giving Martin a keen look.

Martin put down his pen. 'No,' he said defensively. 'He must have told Laura.' He looked up at her. 'You should have mentioned it,' he said in an accusing way.

Laura was stunned at his trying to put the blame for his negligence upon her. 'I——'

Ben interrupted her. 'You are the doctor on this case,' he said to Martin, in a voice like steel. 'It was your duty to question the patient thoroughly. I take it he had a temperature and a headache?' Martin nodded. 'Then it should have been an automatic question. Did you check for neck stiffness? Didn't meningitis enter your head?' He looked at Martin with contempt. 'Hand me the notes. I'll go and see him myself. I know John Greenway's busy.' John was the A and E registrar.

Martin passed the folder to him, his expression chastened. Ben gestured for Laura to precede him out of the office.

He did not speak as they walked towards the cubicle, and Laura wondered if he was blaming her. She wanted to tell him that she had tried to tell Martin about the photophobia but that he had interrupted her, but she couldn't. It seemed like telling tales, somehow.

Colin was lying with his eyes closed, curled up on his side. He opened his eyes reluctantly as Ben and Laura entered. 'I'm Dr Kendricks,' Ben told him quietly. 'I've come to have a look at you.'

'I must go home,' Colin said, trying to sit up. 'My wife's pregnant.'

Ben pressed him back against the pillows. He took a pencil torch from his pocket and said, 'I'd like to have a look at your eyes.'

Colin just sighed. 'Then can I go home?'

Ben lifted Colin's head forward slightly. 'Does your neck hurt?'

Colin frowned. 'No.' He was looking anxiously up at Ben. 'It is just an ear infection, isn't it?'

Ben sat on the bed. 'Yes, but I think we should admit you. This aversion to light and feeling sick means that you are more unwell than you think.' He smiled reassuringly. 'We'll give you an intensive course of antibiotics and keep an eye on you.'

Colin frowned. 'Does keeping an eye on me mean

that I might have meningitis?' His tone was anxious. 'My nephew died of that.'

'I don't think it has come to that,' Ben said. 'But that's why we want to admit you, so that it doesn't.'

'I thought only children get meningitis,' Colin said, frowning.

'Adults can get it if a nasty infection, especially in the ear, isn't treated,' Ben told him.

As Ben rose from the bed Colin grabbed his arm. 'But what about my wife? I live in London and she's pregnant with our first baby.' He was getting agitated.

'Have you some other relatives?' Ben asked kindly.

'My parents live nearby,' Colin said, lying back on the pillow.

'Give Staff their phone number. Sister will let them know and they can look after your wife.' He smiled reassuringly. 'Antibiotics will have you right in no time.'

Laura was impressed by Ben's calm confidence. The atmosphere in the cubicle had been full of apprehension when they had entered, but now it had gone, and Colin had even managed to smile.

How was it that Ben's caring attitude had not extended to David and the baby, Timmy? Laura wondered as he left the cubicle.

Quickly she took the name and address and phone number of Colin's parents and went to the office.

Martin was not there. Ben was telling Celia Jackson about Colin and writing up the notes. 'I'll see he's admitted immediately so that he can start on intravenous fluids and antibiotics right away.' He looked round at Laura. 'Staff has the phone number of his parents, so if you could inform them of his admission, it will help him to stop worrying.'

'I'll do that right away,' Celia said, taking the piece of paper Laura handed to her and entering his parents' information into Colin's notes.

'Right,' Ben said. 'I'll tell John that we've admitted him,' he promised, and left.

'Stay with Mr Bradley, Staff, until the porter can take him up,' Celia said.

Laura did not have to wait long, but while she waited she wondered why Ben had come back to Casualty.

She was late going off duty.

The Accident and Emergency entrance was at the side of the hospital—Ledborough General was an old hospital, but the Accident and Emergency unit had been renovated and extended. It was modern and had the latest equipment.

The hospital was situated on Ledborough Road in the centre of the town. There had been no space for a garden when the hospital had been built originally, but the large house adjacent to it had been acquired by the Local Health Authority when it had become vacant. It had been pulled down and the new Accident and Emergency unit extended. The area was large enough to allow for a small garden, which had been much appreciated by relatives.

Laura stepped from the hospital, her mind occupied with thoughts of how she could quash her attraction to Ben.

She glanced to see if her bus was coming as she passed the garden—the stop was visible from there—

and was surprised to see Rose Powell sitting, head bent, on a bench.

But what she hadn't seen was Ben, talking to Rose a few minutes earlier. That was why he had been in Casualty. He had been passing through to catch Rose before she left.

Ben had found Rose sitting in the garden. He had seen her from the stair window as he walked down from the children's ward on his way to the car park. She had been so deep in thought that he had sat down beside her before she knew it, otherwise she would have fled.

Ben grasped her arm, feeling how thin it was beneath the jacket. Rose looked worn, but more than worn—despairing. That was what Ben had suspected. 'Miss Powell.' His tone was gentle. 'You didn't really drop your baby, did you?'

'What makes you think that?' she said belligerently, trying to pull away.

'I've worked in a hospital in a deprived area. I've seen battered babies, and I don't think yours is.'

Suddenly Rose's stiffness dissolved, and she wept and wept. 'No, I didn't drop him. He did roll off the couch, when I was at the door. I just thought it would be a good idea to imply that I had, then he would be taken from me and given all the things I can't give him.' The words tumbled out.

'That's not the way,' Ben told her. 'It would be on file that you were a mother to watch and any future children that you had would be monitored carefully.' He looked at her kindly. 'You don't want that, do you?'

'I only want what's best for Timmy,' she said pathetically.

'Well, I have a proposition for you,' he said. 'But you'll need to think carefully about it.'

He spoke for some minutes, and when he had finished waited for Rose to reply.

It was a little while before she did so, and then she said, 'I'll think about it.' Her face had lost that despairing look.

Ben rose. 'You do that,' he said, placing a hand on her shoulder and giving it a squeeze before he left.

Rose looked dejected now, and Laura's compassionate nature made her move towards the younger woman. Rose looked up at that moment and, seeing Laura, she sprang to her feet and rushed away.

Laura stood where she was, and in doing so missed her bus. Why had Rose been sitting there? Surely she should have been miles away by now?

CHAPTER FIVE

LAURA was dreading Friday and immersed herself in her work to keep thoughts of Ben away. But, try as she would, she could not keep him out of her thoughts. His kiss had made that impossible. Because he had not touched her before, she had been able to control her attraction to him, but now. . . Now she longed for him to make love to her, and this tormented her. It made her feel guilty.

On Thursday morning, as Laura was going for the bus, she met Audrey Fennel, the girl who lived with her husband in the top flat.

Laura and Sally did not see much of their neighbours except for Audrey, since she worked as a secretary at the hospital. They quite often had lunch together.

'Hi,' Laura said. 'How's the expectant mother? Morning sickness any better?' She was concerned to see how worried Audrey looked.

'I thought at ten weeks it would be better, but it isn't,' Audrey told her despondently, brushing her shoulder-length fair hair behind her ears. She was only five feet three, and looked up at Laura as she said, 'I'm glad I saw you.' A frown wrinkled her forehead. 'I'm a bit worried.'

The bus drew up at that moment and they found all the seats were taken and the aisle almost full of those standing. It was a ten-minute ride to the hospital, but they couldn't speak confidentially in such a crush.

As soon as they had alighted Audrey said, 'I saw a bit of blood this morning. Should I have stayed at home?'

'I think that would have been a good idea,' Laura said, laying her hand on Audrey's arm to prevent the girl going towards the administration block.

'But I haven't had any pain and I'm still on a two-month probation,' Audrey told her, the worry frown deepening on her forehead. 'And if I stay off I might lost this job.'

'I think you should come with me,' Laura said, hiding her concern behind a smile as she led her friend towards the A and E department. 'We'll get a doctor to look at you.'

'But I'll be late for work,' Audrey wailed. 'And they don't know I'm pregnant.'

'The baby is more important, isn't it?' Laura asked kindly, but firmly.

'Yes,' Audrey whispered, and went with Laura unresistingly.

As Laura put her into a cubicle she said, 'They'll have to know some time.' She smiled as she added, 'And I don't think you'll be able to hide it for long.'

Audrey smiled weakly.

'Now just you lie there,' Laura told her as she took off Audrey's shoes and helped her on to the bed. 'We'll get a gynaecologist to see you.' She wrapped the cuff of the blood pressure machine round Audrey's arm. 'But we'll just take your blood pressure, temperature and pulse first.'

They were all normal.

'Do you feel as if you're bleeding now?' Laura asked.

Audrey blushed. 'I put a pad on and it feels a bit damp.'

'I'll bring you another one.'

Laura found Sister in the office and told her about Audrey.

'I'll phone for the duty gynaecologist,' Celia said, lifting the receiver as she ran her finger down the list of doctor's names. 'It's Jane Grant. Stay with the patient until she comes, please, Staff.'

Laura took a clean pad for Audrey and kept the used one which, she was relieved to see, was just stained with blood; there were no clots. The doctor would need to see it.

The gynaecologist came at that moment. 'I'm Jane Grant,' she said with a reassuring smile. She was short, like Audrey, and fair as well, though there were more lines upon her face than showed on the younger woman's. 'Tell me all about it.'

Her manner was so relaxed that Audrey's clenched hands loosened. 'I didn't want to lose my job,' she explained, after she had told Jane about the bleeding. 'There's talk that my husband might be made redundant. He's an electrician. . .' She mentioned a firm that was being taken over. 'It all happened just when I became pregnant, so I got this job.' Tears started to flow.

'Try not to distress yourself,' Jane said, as she gently felt Audrey's abdomen and glanced at the pad. 'I'm sure you won't lost your job, they're short enough of good secretaries and I'll have a word with them.' She smiled reassuringly. 'We'll admit you for a few days to keep an eye on you. Staff will tell your husband.'

'I'll be back in a minute,' Laura said, parting the curtain for Jane to precede her.

Back in the office, Jane said, 'I don't think there's any need to worry, but we'll sedate her and admit her for a few days. Can I use your phone, Celia?'

'Certainly,' Sister said.

Jane informed the ward, then dialled the number of the office where Audrey worked, and explained the situation.

As she replaced the receiver she turned to Laura. 'Tell Audrey her job's safe. They were very understanding.'

Laura knew why Jane Grant was so popular with both staff and patients. She was a very caring person.

Laura hurried to tell Audrey, and was rewarded with a big smile. 'Thanks for helping me,' she said.

That evening, as she sat with Sally to eat their evening meal, Sally asked in a concerned way, 'What's the matter? You're looking awfully peaky.'

Laura finished chewing a piece of ham and salad before she said, 'No, I'm fine. We've been quite busy in A and E, that's all.'

'You'll be even more busy next week, when the schools break up,' said Sally, loading her fork.

Laura groaned. 'If the council cut all the trees down and drained all the ponds and rivers it would make our work much easier.'

Sally laughed. 'You'd have to ban roller-skates and bicycles as well.'

'Poor little things,' Laura said, joining in with her friend's laughter.

They finished their meal and took their coffee into the lounge. 'I'm seeing Ben tomorrow at Thompson and Holgates, the lawyers,' Laura said. 'I'll speak to Mr Thompson about buying the flat then.'

'Fine,' said Sally, looking happy. 'We want to get married in August. No point in waiting. We've waited long enough.'

'Well, I'm sure there won't be any problems,' said Laura.

'What time is your appointment?' Sally asked as she collected the cups.

'At——' Laura's mouth gaped. 'I don't know. I remember telling Ben that it would have to be before three o'clock, as I'm on duty then, but I haven't heard from him since.' She had been so busy trying to keep him out of her thoughts that she had forgotten he had not contacted her.

The phone rang at that moment. Laura picked up the receiver. It was Ben. Almost as if he was answering Sally's question, he said, 'Eleven o'clock at Thompson and Holgates suit you? I can collect you, if you like.'

Laura ran the tip of her tongue over dry lips. 'That'll be fine,' she said, adding rather stiffly, 'But you don't need to collect me.' She would be nervous enough in his company without being enclosed with him in a car.

'Very well.' He rang off.

Ben's off-hand reply disturbed Laura. Just the coolness in his voice upset her and made her feel bereft, and this tormented her all the more.

She still held the receiver, and its continuous buzzing seemed to signify what her life had been like. One continuous straight line with nothing happening. But now. . .

'Hey!' Sally spoke from beside her. 'Can I use the phone?'

'Oh, sorry.' Laura replaced the receiver. 'I'll do the washing-up,' she offered.

If only she could wash all this confusion away as easily as she did the stains on the plates, she mused.

The time until eleven o'clock the next day seemed to drag. She didn't know what to wear. Normally this wasn't a problem, for she had just thrown anything on since David had died.

Looking in her wardrobe, Laura suddenly realised that her indecision was because she was wondering what Ben would like her to wear.

Well, she would stop this right now. She was not going to dress for him. Anyway, she hadn't bought any new clothes yet, so what she had would have to do.

She chose a plain beige skirt with a beige, slightly patterned blouse. A cream cardigan, beige shoes and handbag completed her outfit. Surveying herself in the mirror, she thought how dowdy she looked, and sighed.

Laura's salary had not permitted her to buy a new car and she would not ask Ben for money from David's estate to do so, she reflected as she got behind the wheel of her ancient Metro.

She was ten minutes late due to heavy traffic.

'You should have let me collect you,' Ben said, giving her outfit a cursory glance which hid the desire the sight of her roused in him. She looked fresh and feminine, even if the colours of her clothes were dull.

The sight of Ben, dressed in a light grey suit, white shirt, and university tie—the same university that David had gone to—filled her with such a longing that she could not speak. That it was a longing to feel Ben's touch and not the touch of her dead husband she pushed firmly out of her mind.

The smile left Ben's face when he saw how her expression stiffened.

They were in the lawyer's outer office. 'You can go in now, Dr Kendricks and Mrs Osbourne,' the secretary told them. She was a middle-aged woman, smartly but not sophistically dressed.

'Thanks, Janet,' Ben said, giving her a special smile that Laura thought typical of this man. Any woman warranted a smile from him, she told herself, trying to squash a feeling of jealousy.

But in this she was wrong. There was a reason for Ben's smile. Janet's husband had had a partial gastrectomy, which Ben had performed. It had been an emergency operation.

Hugh Brant had had a gastric ulcer for some time. He was a salesman for the pharmaceutical firm of which Ben's father, Richard Kendricks, was the dynamic head.

Hugh had been waiting in the outer office one day, when Ben had arrived to lunch with his father. Their relationship had improved since the death of Marina Kendricks, Ben's mother, from cancer. Both men had adored the gentle Marina, from whom Ben had inherited his compassion. He did not approve of his father's ruthlessness, partly because he had traces of it in himself, which he had had to curb.

Just as Ben had closed the door behind him Hugh had vomited on to the carpet, the coffee-ground vomit of the bleeding ulcer immediately being recognised by Ben. He had called an ambulance and had gone with Hugh to the London hospital where he had been a junior registrar of some brilliance.

It was the first big operation he had performed under the guidance of the consultant, so he had a special interest in Hugh and his wife, Janet.

'Coming, Laura?' Ben gestured for her to precede him.

'Er, yes.' She was still fighting her jealousy.

She made sure that she did not brush against him as he held the rather narrow door open for her, but as she passed through, she smelt the scent of his aftershave and remembered it from their kiss. It was reminiscent of the sea on a hot summer's day, refreshing and cool. It suited him—all that passion beneath a cool exterior.

'Mrs Osbourne.' James Thompson rose from the desk, hand outstretched. 'This is a pleasure.' He was the senior partner, almost ready for retirement, and his silver hair added to his air of distinction. 'Ben has told me why you're here,' he said, leading her to a chair. 'And I have the papers ready for you both to sign.'

The formalities were completed quickly, and as Laura signed her name, releasing her from Ben's stewardship, she suddenly felt like a ship that had lost its anchor.

She glanced up at Ben, who was standing beside

her chair. He looked so solid and dependable, with
as distinguished an air as the lawyer. It wasn't just
his handsomeness that smote her heart, it was the
essence of him. Here was a man who knew where he
was going. A man whose strength held no doubts.
He followed what he thought to be right, through to
the very end. Laura envied his certainty, even
though it aggravated her. If only he would admit he
had been wrong not to encourage David. If only he
would admit that Timmy needed protection.

He must have sensed her insecurity for he gave
her that kind smile, the one he gave to the patients.
'I'll always be here if you need me,' he said quietly.

Need him? Oh, how she needed him, but not in
quite the way he meant, and because of the need to
fight against the pull he had upon her she said,
'Thanks,' adding, 'But I don't think that will be
necessary now,' the lie almost burning her lips.

The light from the window sharpened the bone-
structure of his face as it stiffened at the sharpness
of her tone and he took a step away from her.

Mr Thompson had been putting papers away in a
cabinet and had not heard the interchange. He
approached them now and went with them to the
door. 'Don't hesitate to call on me for any advice,'
he told Laura.

'Thank you.' The door was open and she was just
about to step through it when she remembered the
flat, and turned back to face him. 'There is something,' she said. 'I would like to buy the flat I share.
My friend owns it and wants to sell.'

'That should pose no problem,' James Thompson

said. 'I have your address and I'll send a surveyor round.'

Laura thanked him and left with Ben, who had waited for her.

On the pavement outside, he glanced at his watch. 'It's only twelve-thirty. How about celebrating the end of our association by lunching with me?' he suggested impulsively, because she was looking vulnerable and stressed.

'Thank you,' Laura accepted. She didn't want to lose the security of his presence just yet—or that was what she told herself.

Ben took her elbow and led her to his car, parked behind the lawyers' office.

As she took her seat, Laura could still feel his touch on her elbow and her hands trembled as she clicked on the seatbelt.

It was hot in the car, but Laura's heat was due to more than the weather. It was sitting so close to Ben that had flushed her with a yearning she struggled to keep in check. She wound down the window.

'The car will soon cool down once we get started,' Ben said.

But will I? wondered Laura.

'I thought we'd have lunch at the Pavilion in the park. They have quite a good menu there and it's too far out for office staff to bother making the journey, so it shouldn't be crowded.'

'Fine,' agreed laura, brightening. It would be lovely in the park today. The roses would be blooming.

They did not speak until Ben drew up in the car park. Laura was glad to escape the tension in the car. She had taken off her cardigan before taking her seat and took it with her when she stepped out.

'Perhaps you should leave your cadigan, then you won't be bothered with it,' Ben suggested.

He was probably right but, just because he was, Laura decided to take it with her. 'I'll just take it,' she said.

Ben shrugged.

A table by the window was just being vacated when they entered. Ben hurried her over to secure it. The restaurant had an atmosphere of the past. It was spacious, with tables of four place-settings, set far enough apart from their neighbours to allow private conversation. The waitresses' uniforms were black with small aprons and they wore caps edged with lace. White damask tableclothes, with napkins to match, the silver place settings and shining glasses gave an impression of a gentler age. It soothed Laura's overstretched nerves.

She was glad their table was by the window. It would give her somewhere to look other than at Ben.

A waitress brought the menu and Laura hid behind it. She wasn't feeling hungry and chose fruit juice and egg salad.

The tension was building inside her as Ben said, 'That's not going to give you much energy to face a busy shift.' He ordered cod mornay and passed the menus to the waitress with a smile.

'I'm not very hungry,' Laura said with a sigh, wishing the smile for the waitress had been for her.

She looked so dejected that Ben wanted to take her into his arms. 'It's a hard time for you,' he said compassionately. 'The end of a period in your life.' He reached for her hand and she didn't withdraw it.

'Yes,' she whispered, close to tears, not surprised that he understood. He was intuitive. But what he did not understand was that it was the end of her association with him that was causing her pain.

This should have pleased her, feeling the way she did about his professional behaviour, but it didn't. She just felt an unbearable longing to be taken into his arms and to stay there forever.

It was then she realised that she loved him, had always loved him from the first moment they had met, that she had suppressed this because she had loved David and had been married to him.

But her love for David had been different from the love she felt for Ben. There had been no discord between David and herself, no fiery passion, as she knew there would be between herself and Ben.

Knowing that there was too much between them that was unsolvable, she fought the despair she was feeling and said in a bright way, 'But I intend to go forward now. Live life as it should be lived, as fully as possible.'

'Good for you,' he said, smiling.

Ridiculously pleased, she returned his smile, and the tension left her so that she was able to chat generally with some success throughout the rest of the meal.

As they left the table and made their way towards the exit a voice said, 'Hello, Ben.'

Too wrapped in their own thoughts, they had not seen Bea Nicholson, who was lunching with a lady who was obviously her mother; the resemblance was marked. Bea was looking smart in a sleeveless dress, its blue colour exactly matching her eyes. Laura wished she had made an effort and bought her new clothes. She felt even more dowdy.

'I'll be ready at seven-thirty this evening,' Bea said, smiling into Ben's eyes, ignoring Laura.

'I'll look forward to that,' Ben assured her.

So that was why the childrens' ward sister had treated her so coldly and was looking at her coolly now. Bea was interested in Ben, and he seemed to reciprocate the interest, judging by the admiring look in his eye. Well, it was only natural that a red-blooded man like Ben should have a woman friend. Or was Bea his lover?

As they left the restaurant, Ben said, 'I'll run you back to your car.'

'No, thanks.' Laura was adamant. Perhaps a spell in the peacefulness of the park would calm her and allow her to put her thoughts into perspective.

'All right,' said Ben, but he did not leave, just walked beside her as she turned away.

Laura frowned. 'I'd like to be on my own,' she said sharply.

'Oh, I don't think that's a good idea,' he said, ignoring her tone.

Laura came to a halt. 'Isn't that just like you?' she said, a flash of anger in her tone. 'Always think you know best.'

'Yes,' Ben laughed, then he became serious. 'I wanted to talk to you away from people.' There was no one about and they were standing so still that a small bird hopped quite close to them. Ben took a step nearer to her. 'I want to know if there's a place in this new life of yours for me?' he asked softly, his eyes dark with desire.

'Maybe,' she whispered, forgetting her recent despair as his compelling eyes held hers.

He moved even closer, so that their clothes touched. The next moment he had pulled her into his arms and his mouth came down upon hers in a demanding kiss.

Her body leapt into life and she was powerless to prevent his kiss deepening, her body from melting, her senses from flaring.

Her arms went round his neck and tightened, pulling him closer, longing for the ultimate, intimate closeness. But with this longing came a terrible thought. Had her marriage to David been a lie?

She wrenched herself from him, and as he reached for her again, his eyes now wild with desire, she held up her hand and retreated from him. 'No. There can never be a "maybe" between us, Ben.' She was trembling with unfulfilment.

'You can't deny this——' his face was tight with intensity '—this thing between us.' His voice was hoarse with desire as he took a step towards her.

'There's too much. . .' Her voice deserted her and she spread her hands, tears running down her face, before she turned and fled from him, leaving him feeling as tormented as she was.

CHAPTER SIX

LAURA was just walking into A and E on Saturday when Martin caught up with her. She had spent a dreadful night, tormented with unfulfilled desire. When she had fallen asleep, she'd dreamt of David's trusting face smiling at her and had awoken feeling like a wife who had been unfaithful.

'Lovers' tiff?' Martin asked, seeing the misery and strain in her face.

'Lover?' Laura's mind was still on the guilt she had awoken with.

'Ben Kendricks.'

'He is not my lover,' she snapped. 'He was just the executor of my husband's estate, but he isn't any longer.'

Martin's eyes brightened. 'Ohhh. Well, in that case. . .'

'What case?' Ben joined them.

'Nothing,' Martin said hurriedly, and quickly left them.

'What was all that about?' Ben asked.

'Nothing,' Laura repeated Martin's word. 'How's Robert?' she asked in her best professional voice, to keep a longing to touch Ben at bay. He was looking as ragged as she must be.

'I was worried he would develop a rip-roaring infection after his appendix burst on the table when I was operating,' he told her, taking his tone from hers. 'He's been pretty poorly since, though mostly due to his debilitated state.' The worry lines on his face did not clear as he added, 'We infused him and filled him with antibiotics, which seem to have controlled the infection, but he's not picking up as well as I would have wished.' They were standing at the entrance to A and E as they spoke. 'Perhaps a visit from you would cheer him up,' Ben suggested, and added with a strained smile, 'I know it would me.'

The thought of Ben lying sick was intolerable and caused her to say softly, before she could stop herself, 'Then I promise to visit if you are.' She immediately regretted it when she saw Ben's eyes burn with desire.

'However, there's good news about Colin Bradley. The massive doses of antibiotic have stopped him getting meningitis,' Ben told her curtly, the regret he saw in her face dampening his ardour.

'Oh, that is good news,' she said, over brightly.

'Yes, isn't it?' There was a touch of sarcasm in his voice.

He turned and left her, and as Laura watched him go she felt as if part of her went with him.

That afternoon, Laura visited Robert on her way off duty. 'How are you today?' she asked as she put a bottle of orange squash down on his locker-top.

'Fine,' he replied, giving her a tight smile. 'And thanks for the squash.'

Laura suspected that he was anything but fine. He was depressed. She drew a chair close to the bed and sat down. 'Won't you let me contact your parents?' she asked.

'No!' His tone was adamant.

'But your mother——'

'She'd only want me to come home.' He frowned in distress. 'I can't do that.'

'Can't do what?' asked Ben, placing his hands on to Laura's shoulders to press her back into the chair as she made to rise. She hadn't heard him approach.

'Nothing,' said Robert quickly.

Ben did not persist. He removed his hands, which had lingered just a little longer than was necessary, and her shoulders felt naked without his touch.

'How are you today?' Ben asked, repeating Laura's question as he flicked through the notes he had brought with him.

'Fine.' Robert gave the same reply as he had to Laura.

He was the senior registrar and she was a nurse, so Laura felt she had to ask, 'Can I help you?' even though she was out of uniform.

Ben glanced around. 'I did have a nurse when I left the office, but she seems to have disappeared. It was that dizzy blonde who seems to be on this ward now.'

A moment later Michelle Pearson came hurrying up the ward. 'Sorry, Doctor. . .' Her hand flew to her mouth. 'Oh, I'm sorry—Mr Kendricks.' She used the surgeon's proper title. 'I went back for the notes.'

Ben waved them. 'I have them.'

'Oh.' Michelle looked embarrassed.

Ben smiled. 'I'm sure you won't mind if Staff stays instead of you, will you?'

'Oh, no,' Michelle said hurriedly.

Laura glanced at Robert and, seeing his look of disappointment, guessed that he would mind. The stressed lines on his face had softened when he looked at the fair nurse, but Laura couldn't countermand Ben's request. He was the doctor.

'Come back in a minute or two, Nurse,' Laura said kindly.

'Yes, Staff.' Michelle gave Robert a gentle smile and left.

Ben raised an eyebrow at Laura. 'I do have other patients to see, Staff.'

Laura was surprised at the sharpness of his tone. His politeness towards the staff was well known. Perhaps it was just the tenseness between them that had caused it.

Her expression must have shown her thoughts, for he said, 'I was up half the night.'

'Oh, yes.'

Laura had heard about the accident case that had been brought in in the small hours. So that was why he was looking so tired, and not through emotional exhaustion as she was.

'Staff!' Ben's tone was sharp.

Laura jumped. 'Sorry,' she said, and felt she sounded like Michelle.

Ben gave her an exasperated look before turning to Robert and saying, 'I just want to examine you.'

Laura drew the curtains round the bed and turned down the sheet. Robert undid his pyjamas.

Gently, Ben felt Robert's abdomen. The teenager winced. 'Still sore?'

'Yes,' Robert said. 'Shouldn't I be better by now, with all the antibiotics I've had?'

'Your run-down condition hasn't helped. I'm afraid we'll have to keep you here a bit longer.'

'In case the infection flares up again,' Robert said.

Ben looked at him in surprise, though not Laura. She knew Robert had dropped out of medical school. 'Yes,' Ben agreed.

'I was studying medicine,' Robert explained in a small voice.

'Ahhh!' Ben looked at him thoughtfully. 'Perhaps being a patient might encourage you to take it up again.'

'Oh, no. I couldn't compete——' Robert gave a small gasp and didn't continue.

Ben decided to ignore this and said, 'Well, all you have to do is to concentrate on getting better.'

Robert's tight face relaxed. 'I'll try.'

'Perhaps Nurse Pearson can help you?' Ben suggested with a grin.

Robert blushed.

Michelle had been hovering close by. Laura beckoned her over as she drew the curtains back from the bed. 'Try and get him to let his parents know he's here,' she said in a quiet voice as Michelle joined them.

'I will,' Michelle promised.

'What did you think of Robert's talk of not being able to compete?' Ben asked Laura as they left the bed.

'Perhaps his father's a doctor?' she suggested.

'And perhaps Wilson isn't his real surname. A medical student just starting wouldn't know about recurrent infection.'

'You're right,' Laura said, feeling that niggle of annoyance his being right always gave her.

'Perhaps you could do some detective work?' He glanced back towards Robert's bed. Michelle was helping him to have a drink. 'Nurse Pearson's the answer. I think we should discuss it.'

'I don't think that's necessary——' Laura began to protest, but Ben had taken her arm and pulled her into an empty side-ward. 'Neither do I,' he said huskily, his eyes flaring with desire. 'I could hardly work last night for thinking of you.'

His voice was urgent and Laura felt powerless to reply, in the grip of an emotion so strong she felt faint with the force of it. Memories of his love-making yesterday were still with her. She would have fallen if his strong hands had not reached for her and swept her into his arms.

'I. . .' The word whispered from her, but his mouth came down upon hers in a kiss that prevented speech, that prevented thought. The tumultuous feelings started by his kiss yesterday surged through her body.

It had never been like this with David—this eagerness, this longing to feel his bare flesh pressed against hers, this fever of excitement, this not caring who came in and saw them in a passionate embrace.

'Laura, Laura,' Ben whispered against her mouth. 'I have wanted you for so long.'

She didn't hear his words. All she knew was that he had lifted his lips from hers, and a small cry left her. She was like a child who had had something precious taken away from it. Laura wanted that binding that a kiss made between them, wanted to stay in this world of pleasure and delight.

Then, as he kissed her again, more deeply, Laura wanted more; she wanted everything, she wanted the final fulfilment. She didn't think that her life with David had been a lie, but her desire for Ben was too strong.

It was he who finally pulled them apart. Her hair was awry, her blouse and skirt crushed, but she did not see any of this. She just saw Ben, big powerful and strong, and felt even more frustrated than she had yesterday.

'You. . . You. . .' The torment of unfulfilled desire was clear in her eyes, but he misread it.

'David is dead and we're alive,' he said harshly, gripping her by the arms and shaking her. 'You can't deny yourself any longer. You want me as much as I want you and have always done so.' Passion was still etched in his face, inches from hers. 'Don't you?' He shook her again. 'Don't you?' He was almost shouting.

'Yes. Damn you! Yes, yes, yes.' She shook her head, as if to deny what she was saying, her eyes filled with confusion and distress and sudden tears. To have it put into words that she had always wanted him, even when she was married to David, brought back her guilt a hundred fold.

She couldn't stay a moment longer. Bending, she picked up her shoulder-bag, which she did not remember dropping, straightened her clothes and fled from the room. Will I always be running away from him? her heart cried. But is it he I'm running away from? Isn't it myself?

Laura rushed as quickly as she dared down the stairs, rather than take the lift in her dishevelled state. She glanced out of the window that over-looked the car park to see if Ben's car was there and saw Rose Powell sitting in the garden on the same seat as she had before.

Laura stopped on the landing of the first floor, her pounding heart steadying. Why was Rose there? Now calmer, Laura was still pondering this when she reached the ground floor, just as the lift doors opened and Ben stepped out.

'Rose Powell's in the vistors' garden,' she said, her professional curiosity overcoming her wish to flee from him.

'Why shouldn't she be?' Ben said tensely.

'But why is she here? Is she visiting someone?'

'Why don't you ask her?' he said irritably.

'You know why she's here,' Laura accused him.

'Yes.' They were standing in the entrance hall of the hospital, glaring at each other.

'Why aren't you telling me, then?' She was annoyed.

'Ever heard of the Hippocratic oath?' he asked sarcastically.

Laura couldn't understand why he sounded so bitter. 'Yes. It's where doctors and nurses are not allowed to betray a patient's confidence. But it doesn't apply in this case.'

Much as she did not want to detain him, her desire to know was stronger. Something deep inside her was nagging her to persist. She put a hand on his arm to delay him. 'But——'

'But, nothing,' he said sharply. 'If you want to

know you'll have to ask her, not me.' He pulled his arm from her grasp and strode away.

As Laura passed the garden, Rose was hurrying towards her. 'Have you just come from the children's ward?' she asked, her green eyes haunted.

'No,' Laura said, with sudden compassion for the stricken face before her. 'I work in Casualty.'

'Oh, I forgot,' Rose said. 'It was seeing you take Timmy to the ward that made me think you worked there.' She turned away, her head bowed.

Laura caught up with her. 'I'm sure it will be all right if you want to see him,' she said eagerly. 'It's open visiting on the children's ward.'

'No,' Rose said sharply, and quickened her step. 'It would be too difficult to make up my mind if I did.'

As Laura walked beside her, she suddenly realised that Rose loved her son. She grasped the other woman's arm. 'There's a café over the road. How about a cup of tea?'

'You don't want to have tea with me,' Rose said bitterly, but she didn't pull away.

'Come on.' Laura linked her arm in Rose's so that she couldn't bolt.

The café was sparse, with wooden chairs and tables covered with plastic cloths. A bottle of tomato ketchup, brown sauce, pepper and salt stood in the centre of each table, with a bowl of sugar. The place was clean and served a variety of dishes, mostly accompanied with chips.

'What'll you have?' Laura asked, suspecting that Rose's slimness was due to lack of food rather than dieting. She was not wearing jeans, T-shirt and leather jacket today, but a blue cotton skirt with a white blouse. Rose's clothes were clean, but well worn. Her hair was not spiked now, but combed into a cap-like fashion, close to her head. She looked young and vulnerable.

'Just a cup of tea, thanks,' Rose said, but her eyes lingered on the pies that could be heated in a microwave.

Laura went up to the counter and ordered two pies and chips with beans, and a pot of tea. She wasn't hungry herself, but didn't want to make Rose uncomfortable by not eating with her.

'I didn't ask for that,' Rose objected strongly as Laura put the dishes down on the table.

'Well, I'm hungry,' Laura lied. 'And I don't like eating alone.' She smiled at the belligerent face, then her smile turned to compassion as Rose's eyes filled with tears. Quickly she sat down. 'Here,' she pushed the plate towards Rose and poured a cup of tea. 'Have a drink.' Tears dropped into Rose's tea as she did as she was told. 'Tell me about it,' Laura said kindly.

A big sigh escaped Rose's lips. 'That doctor who saw Timmy when I first brought him in caught me in the garden.' That must have been when I saw her, thought Laura, but did not interrupt. 'He said that the Social Services and the health visitor had told them that I was a good mother and could not possibly hurt Timmy.' She took another gulp of tea, but left her meal untouched.

Laura was thrilled to find that she had been mistaken where Ben was concerned. He had done something about Timmy. But why was Rose so distressed? And what had she meant when she'd said that visiting Timmy would make making up her mind too difficult?

Laura didn't speak, she just looked sympathetic. Tears fell again down Rose's cheeks and dropped on to her pie. She sniffed, and Laura delved in her bag for a tissue and handed it to the stricken mother. Rose used it and sighed.

'Have something to eat while it's hot,' Laura encouraged. 'Then you can tell me the rest.'

They ate in silence until their plates were empty. After finishing her cup of tea, Rose said, 'When Timmy fell off the couch, I suddenly thought of a way for him to have all the things I couldn't give him. I just don't have the cash, and I was getting desperate, and as he's so young I can't leave him and get a job.' She took a deep breath. 'So I decided if they thought I had deliberately injured him, they would take him into care.'

Laura reached for Rose's hand and, as she did so, it reminded her of how Ben had taken hers in the Pavilion café. 'But you would have been taken to court, and it would have been on record for the rest of your life,' Laura said quietly.

Rose pulled her hand away. 'That's what Dr Kendricks said when he had a chat with me. He asked if there was a relative who could take Timmy, but I told him there wasn't. My sister has six of her own and is struggling to survive with an out-of-work husband.'

Rose sighed. 'It was then that he suggested adoption. I hadn't thought of that.' A worried frown creased her brow. 'He said he could put me in touch with a voluntary adoption agency run by his cousin and explained how these, and the local government agencies, take into account what sort of qualities a mother would like in adoptive parents.' Rose's face brightened a little as she spoke. 'It's not everybody who can have their parents chosen for them, is it?'

Laura smiled, but did not speak.

A look of pain entered Rose's eyes. 'He said I should think about it.' Her shoulders sagged.

Laura felt tears prick at her eyes. What a sacrifice to make. She didn't think she would have been able to do the same, similarly situated. What could she say that would not sound patronising or presumptuous?

After a pause for thought she said, 'Is there any hope of you marrying the father?'

'No, none,' Rose said vehemently. 'I never want to see him again.' She shuddered. 'He was married and didn't tell me until I told him I was pregnant, then he didn't want to know.'

Laura detected a vulnerability beneath the force of Rose's denial and her sympathy deepened. Poor Rose. She was still in love with the heel. 'Well. . .' Laura paused again. 'A child needs a secure upbringing, preferably in a home with a loving father and a mother,' she suggested gently.

Rose had been making circles with her fork in a patch of tea that had been spilt from the pot. She put her fork on the plate and looked at Laura. 'Yes. I hadn't thought of that.' Her troubled face cleared. 'It would be great for Timmy.'

'How old are you, Rose?' Laura asked.

'Eighteen.'

'Have you any training of any sort?'

'No. I worked in a pub. That's where I met Ken.'

'Is that what you want to do?' Laura asked.

'No.' She blushed. 'I'd like to be a nurse.'

'You'd have to do your general training, then.'

'I got some exams, including biology,' Rose said eagerly.

'Well, then.' Laura was excited for her. 'I think you should apply. She pulled paper and pen from her bag and wrote the name and address of the nursing officer at the nurses' training college in Ledborough and passed it to Rose. 'That's who you apply to for an application form when you're ready.'

The eagerness left Rose's face. 'Yes, well. I suppose adoption would be the best thing for Timmy.'

'And for you,' Laura said gently. 'You could make a new life for yourself.'

'I suppose so.'

Laura's heart went out to the despondent girl. 'I'll give you my address. Let me know how you get on.' Laura scribbled her name and address on the same paper.

'Thanks.' Rose took it from her.

Laura went with Rose to the bus stop and waited with her until her bus came. 'Thanks,' Rose said as she boarded the bus.

Laura stood and watched until it turned the corner. A few drops of rain roused her. Poor Rose, she thought, as she started to walk in the direction of her home.

A car drew up beside her and a voice said, 'Want a lift, lady?' It was Ben.

'Thanks.'

His expression showed his surprise. 'I suppose you took this lift because it's raining?' he said sarcastically.

As Laura snapped on the seatbelt she said, 'No. I've been speaking to Rose and want to apologise. This gives me the opportunity.'

'Oh?' Ben had his head turned away from her as he looked over his shoulder at the oncoming traffic before moving out. Once they were on their way, though, he said, 'I hope you didn't make one of your snap judgements and dissuade her from adoption?'

'Now who's making a snap judgement?' Laura said crossly.

'Sorry,' he said. 'It's been a trying day, in more ways than one.'

'Meaning me, I suppose?' she said.

'Not altogether.' Ben turned into her road and drew up outside her flat.

Laura made no move to leave the car. 'I'm sorry I criticised you,' she said. 'It was very kind of you to explain to Rose about the adoption agencies. I didn't say very much, really. I just listened and suggested that Timmy might be better with a family.' She looked straight at Ben. 'But won't she regret her decision later?' Her hazel eyes were troubled.

'Perhaps. I don't know.' He sounded weary, then he touched her anxious face. 'If you take people's troubles to heart like this you'll be burnt out before you're thirty,' he said with a smile.

I wish you wouldn't touch me, she thought, longing to catch hold of his hand and kiss it. 'Can you care too much?' she asked, to distract her thoughts from wanting him.

'Sometimes,' he said softly. 'You still care for David.'

But it's not David now, it's you, she longed to tell him. But the guilty thought that she might not have loved her husband was still with her. 'Yes,' she said, vehemently, to convince herself, and as soon as she had said it she knew it was true, and the relief this knowledge brought her brought with it the blame she laid on Ben. 'And I still care that I could have had longer with him if you had encouraged him to take chemotherapy.' The words tumbled out.

'So you still blame me?' He had been leaning forward to kiss her, but now he jerked back, his face stiff with shock. 'I thought that was in the past when you responded to my kisses.' He looked bewildered.

'To my shame,' she said, wanting to hurt him as much as she was hurting. 'I fight against this attraction for you, but. . .'

He leant forward and flung open the door. 'You won't need to any more,' he said grimly.

Laura almost fell from the car, and watched through tear-filled eyes as he drove away.

She let herself into the flat, feeling desolate.

CHAPTER SEVEN

Two days later Laura was on night duty, and glad of it. When Ben had been in London her contact with him had been minimal, but here in the hospital it was almost impossible to avoid him. She'd see him passing through A and E, or in the canteen, or in the corridor, or catch a glimpse of him driving away and wouldn't admit that she was actively looking for him.

Alone in the staff-room, Laura snatched a quick cup of coffee at eleven o'clock. Linda Connolly, the night A and E sister, had gone off sick with severe tonsillitis, so Laura was in charge. Like most of the nurses, Linda had come on duty at nine, but had had to go home again, too ill to work. Laura was delighted that Sally had been sent to A and E to help. She also was doing night duty, as she was working her month's notice.

Laura was just washing her mug when Martin came in.

'Have you a partner for the university's summer ball?' he asked as he poured a cup of coffee and brought it over to where she was standing at the sink. Ledborough University invited the staff of the general hospital to its summer ball every year.

'Uh?' Laura asked, absentmindedly. The window at the sink overlooked the car park and Laura was looking to see if Ben's car was still there. It was. She had noticed it when she came on at nine and wished she could stop being obsessed with him.

'The summer dance?' Martin repeated irritably.

Her thoughts still on Ben, Laura answered vaguely, 'No.'

'Then you'll go with me?' Martin asked eagerly.

'Go where?' Laura asked irritably, wondering what he was going on about.

'Really, Laura——' Martin didn't bother to hide his aggravation '—stop going around in a dream. Ben Kendricks isn't interested in you now that he no longer has to handle your affairs.'

This sharpened Laura's mind dramatically. She twisted round from the sink. 'What do you know about that?' she asked angrily.

'You told me—don't you remember?' Martin asked in an aggrieved tone.

'I never di——' Her mouth hung open. Then she remembered mentioning that Ben's stewardship was finished the day after the visit to the lawyers.

'See,' he said, pleased like a child that was right.

'Yes, I do see,' Laura said in a resigned way. She saw that she would have to convince Martin that she was not interested in him all over again, and felt like groaning.

'I know for a fact that he's taking Bea.'

'Oh!'

'Well?'

'I suppose so,' she said dejectedly.

'Well, you might show a bit more enthusiasm.'

He was looking so hurt as he put his empty cup down that Laura took pity on him and linked her arm in his. 'Yes, you're right. It was rude of me.'

She regretted her impulse immediately when he squeezed her arm to his side and said, 'I'll make sure you have a good time, I promise,' almost leering down at her.

That was what she was afraid of. She knew he wouldn't leave her side. It had happened at the Christmas dance, to which, in her apathy, she had also let him take her.

Laura extricated her arm. 'Have to go,' she said airily. 'Duty calls.'

She slipped out of the staff-room, but she wasn't quick enough. She had just closed the door when it opened and Martin was beside her. 'I'm going that way,' he said, linking his arm through hers this time.

It was this picture of chumminess that Ben saw as they came into the main area of A and E, and he was shocked at the jealousy that tore at him.

Laura was trying to pull her arm free, but Martin had it clamped to his side too tightly. When she saw Ben, though, she stopped struggling, and deliberately smiled up at Martin.

That she was using Martin, this time to protect herself from her awareness of Ben, as she had used Ben to put Martin off at Sally's birthday party, made her feel uncomfortable. What sort of a woman was she?

Laura felt even more uncomfortable when she glanced up at Martin and saw the adoration in his eyes.

'I need you, Staff,' Ben said sharply, in his registrar's voice. 'Perhaps you could indulge in such intimacies in your off-duty?'

That was a big strong, she thought. 'Intimacies',

indeed. Then just the word set her imagination flying, with pictures of herself and Ben in a really intimate situation, where his hands were inflaming her body, and she blushed.

Anger at having blushed made her say, 'You can talk,' as she remembered him kissing her in the men's surgical side-ward.

Ben's face became grim. 'This is a hospital,' he said, and an ambulance siren sounded, as if to reinforce his words.

Martin pulled his arm reluctantly from Laura's, saying, 'I'll phone you.' She nodded her assent.

As he left them, Laura asked, in a cool tone, 'What is it you want?'

'Want? I want to get you into bed,' he told her harshly, his flesh suddenly burning with desire as he saw her pink tongue moisten lips that had become dry when she'd seen the sudden flash of desire in his eyes and had had to fight to prevent it showing in her own.

Ben didn't need a staff nurse. He was just passing through A and E on his way home, as he found himself doing more often these days, in the hope of catching a glimpse of Laura.

When he'd seen her so intimate with Martin he had wanted to tear her from him, and had said, in his registrar's voice, the only thing that would do it.

Her eyes opened with shock at the bluntness of his words and she said bitingly, 'Well, that's just your tough luck.' And mine too, a voice inside her whispered.

They were standing glaring at each other, near the office, when the door opened and John Greenway came out. 'Ah! Just the person I need,' he said, seeing Ben. 'And you too, Staff.'

John was a big man, with red hair and a round, cheerful face. He was married with six children, and Laura often wondered how he looked so unharassed. His wife, Eileen, was also a calm person. Must be because they're so happy, Laura had decided, when she had done some babysitting for them in their chaotic house. Their children ranged in ages from twelve down to the baby of six weeks. They were a lively bunch, but well-disciplined.

'Accident cases are coming in. That ambulance siren is probably heralding them now.'

Sally appeared at his shoulder. 'Yes. It sounds like it,' she said.

Neither of them seemed to notice the tension between Laura and Ben.

'I was just going home,' Ben said complainingly.

John laughed. 'What have you been doing till this hour?' He gave Ben a sly look. 'Running after the nurses?'

'No.' His tone was sharp. 'Doing some reading for a paper I'm writing.'

'OK, OK.' John saw the bleakness on the couple's faces. 'We could do with your help, though,' he said. 'It sounds a nasty one.' He frowned. 'Two teenagers. One had just passed his test and was driving too fast. The car went out of control and crashed into another car with a couple in it. The man was killed, according to the radio message we got. But the woman's still alive.'

'What about the teenagers?' asked Ben. He was the professional now.

'The driver was killed and his mate's in a bad way.'

The noise of rushing footsteps and trolley wheels drew their attention. The calming green of the paramedics' uniforms was not reflected on the faces of the men. Tense urgency was etched there as they pushed the two trolleys carrying their patients into the accident and emergency department.

Laura could see the airway in place through the clear oxygen mask covering the woman's face.

Susan Hadley, who was in Casualty as part of her training, hurried forward. 'A man's just come in with nasty burns to his legs. He collapsed with the shock of it and by the time someone found him his legs had blistered, and now the blisters have burst, sticking his trousers to the burns. He's a night porter at the hotel over the road.' She gestured in its direction.

'You go and see to him, Martin,' John instructed, as Martin reappeared.

Probably glad to go, thought Laura. She suspected that he did not really like casualty work. 'Nurse Baxter will help you,' Laura called after him.

Within minutes, the two staff nurses and Susan Hadley joined the medical team in the emergency resuscitation room. Two accident trolleys were positioned in the centre of the floor, with enough working space between them.

These trolleys were specially constructed to tilt the head down when necessary, with cot sides to snap up to prevent the patient from falling off. There were also holders for intravenous infusions, oxygen and a back-rest.

All the equipment required in an accident unit to treat major injuries and to resuscitate was within reach. X-ray-viewing boxes, working surfaces, cupboards containing dressing packs, prepacked gauze, pads, syringes, needles and other items, as well as boxes of gloves, which, since the advent of AIDS, all doctors and staff wore when doing any treatments.

The ECG monitor and suction machines were all within reach of the accident trolleys, as were the anaesthetic machine, airway equipment and chest drainage kits. Intravenous infusion equipment, dressing and suturing material and emergency drugs were close by on another trolley. Theatre lights provided the bright light so necessary to see how badly injured the patients were.

The woman, of about thirty, and the teenage passenger were lifted on to the trolleys.

'You take the woman, Ben,' John said, as he looked down at the injured teenager. The boy also had an airway in and oxygen was being given from a portable set.

'Question the ambulancemen before they go, will you Nurse?' Laura asked Susan as she helped lift the woman on to the trolley. 'Get as many details as you can about the accident and the relatives, and look in her handbag for her name and write out a name-tape for her.'

As soon as the patient was on the trolley, Laura started to cut the seams of the woman's clothes. It was imperative to see just what injuries lay beneath the T-shirt and jeans. She covered the patient with a cellular blanket when she had finished.

As she worked she could hear the ambulanceman saying, 'It was a shambles when we arrived. The driver of the family car was dead, the whole of that side of the car crushed and most of the other side as well. The lady was unconscious, and we put up a drip and managed to insert an airway.' He sighed. 'The other car was even more damaged. We were lucky to be able to get them out without the fire brigade's help. The driver was dead, with multiple injuries, and his friend was badly injured.'

He rubbed a hand across his forehead before continuing. 'He managed to tell us before he lost consciousness that his friend had just passed his test that day. He had tried to tell his pal he was driving too fast in a built-up area, but the boy was too excited to listen and the car went out of control.' He sighed again. 'You never get used to seeing broken bodies,' he said sadly.

Laura saw that her patient was still looking grey, in spite of the oxygen. Ben was checking the drip. 'Good job they managed to put it up before her veins collapsed,' he said. 'We'll be lucky if we can get blood from her now.'

Although the patient did not show any signs of bleeding, blood would be taken for grouping and cross-matching immediately. It might be needed later.

A sphygmomanometer cuff had been applied to the upper arm and tightened. Quickly Ben cleaned the skin of the hand near the wrist and inserted a venflon needle, strapped it down with micropore, then took the blood. Laura released the cuff as soon as the blood was taken. The duty lab technician took it immediately to the laboratory.

Susan snapped the name-tape on to the patient's wrist. 'Her name's Lydia Grover,' she told Laura.

Ben examined the patient, exposing her as little as possible as he did so. There didn't appear to be anything wrong with her apart from her head injury. 'Her pupils react to light,' he said. 'So that's a good sign.' He looked in her ears and nose. 'No sign of bleeding from there.' If there had been, he would have suspected a brain haemorrhage. He then listened to her chest. 'Everything seems normal there, except that her heart rate's up. What's her blood pressure doing?'

'Dropping,' Laura said, also frowning.

Ben turned the blanket back a bit more to show the abdomen. Laura put Lydia's T-shirt over her chest so that she was not too exposed. 'It might just be shock,' he said, and at that moment Lydia Grover regained consciousness, pulled off the mask and coughed out the airway.

'You're all right,' Laura hurried to reassure her before she could panic. 'You've had an accident and are in hospital.' She smiled reassuringly. 'Can you tell us if anything hurts?'

Lydia raised a hand to her forehead. She was a pretty woman, with regular features and dark hair. 'My head,' she muttered, then her dazed eyes looked at Laura. 'There was an accident. My husband. . .' Lines of anxiety creased her forehead.

What could Laura say? To tell her patient that her husband had been killed could make her condition worse. She was about to say something non-commital when Ben said, 'He's not at this hospital.' Which was true, in a way. He was in the morgue, which was separate from the building.

'Oh.'

Ben was looking at Lydia's abdomen. There was something wrong. It seemed too swollen. He blew on his hands to warm them and then gently palpated her. 'You're not pregnant, are you?' he asked.

'No,' whispered Lydia.

'Does that hurt?' Ben asked.

Laura knew Ben was hiding what he suspected behind an impassive face. Something *was* wrong. She watched as his fingers touched Lydia's skin, but did not imagine them touching her own this time. She was too concerned for her patient.

The abdomen looked tense, and that combined with the pulse which was rising, the blood pressure that was dropping and the signs of increasing shock—pallor, sweating and air hunger—caused Laura to suspect her patient was bleeding internally.

This was confirmed when Ben said quietly, 'We'll have to take you to Theatre, Mrs. . .' He glanced at Laura.

'Grover,' she told him.

'Mrs Grover. I think you might have a little tear inside.'

Lydia did not seem interested and Laura wondered if her patient realised the significance of what Ben had said. She was probably too concussed.

Ben nodded to Laura who said, 'I'm just going to tip the top of the trolley downwards a bit.'

He beckoned to Laura after she had adjusted the trolley. 'She's haemorrhaging,' he said when they

were out of the patient's hearing. We'll need to get
her to Theatre right away.'

He was the efficient calm surgeon.

'I don't think she really understands. Probably too
concussed,' he said, confirming Laura's thought.
'Try and get her to understand and sign a consent
form. I'll alert the theatre. We'll just give her some
atropine, that's all.'

Laura sent the auxiliary nurse to fetch the porter.

Ben had just phoned Theatre to alert them and
was replacing the receiver when John joined him.
'Something up?' he asked.

Ben told him what he suspected as he wrote up
the atropine.

'Good job you were here,' John said with a smile.

'You could look at it like that, I suppose,' Ben
agreed.

The amused interchange might have shocked a lay
person, but little bursts of humour helped the medical staff defuse the tension they were under.

He handed the notes to Laura without glancing at
her, and hurried off to the theatre. Laura and Sally
check the atropine for her. By the time it was given,
a porter had arrived with a trolley and the staff
carefully removed Lydia from the accident trolley
on to it.

'Will you take the patient to Theatre, please,
Sally?' Laura asked.

Sally nodded, and left with the trolley.

Ben had already gone, but John was still there.
Laura had been so involved with Lydia that she
hadn't noticed what was happening at the other
accident trolley.

When she saw a screen had been put round it she didn't need to ask, but John saw her glance and said, 'We lost him, I'm afraid.' He took a deep breath. 'He had severe injuries—multiple fractures, including a fracture of the skull.' He gave a big sigh. 'Perhaps it was as well,' he said. 'He wouldn't have had much quality of life if he had survived. Probably have been paralysed and like a vegetable as well.'

Laura could see how stressed he was. It was never easy to lose a patient, even if the doctor knew, as in this case, that the patient's survival would have had tragic consequences. 'How about a cup of tea?' she suggested sympathetically.

'Good idea.' He smiled, but the smile did not take the sadness from his eyes.

'What shall I do with this?' Susan asked, her eyes big in a small face as she showed Laura Lydia's handbag.

Susan looked stressed as well, and Laura could remember feeling the same when she attended her first severe accident case.

'We'll take it to Reception,' she said, putting an arm round the girl's shoulders. 'They'll lock it away until it can be returned to the patient, or her relatives.'

They were lucky that it was not a Friday or Saturday night, when A and E was usually busy with drunks and fight victims. They had more time for the little things, like comforting a nurse on her first night in Casualty.

It was almost one o'clock when they sat to drink their tea, the paperwork completed. Martin came in to the office with Winifred Baxter, a state-enrolled nurse of thirty with considerable experiences.

'That burn will need to go to Theatre for washing and dressing—too painful without an anaesthetic,' said Martin. 'Apparently he turned quickly and his elbow caught a kettle of boiling water, knocking it over his legs.' Martin sounded irritated.

John put down his cup. 'I'm sure he didn't do it on purpose,' he said sarcastically.

Martin reddened, but did not say anything.

'What have you done with him?' John asked.

'Given him a shot of pethidine and put a sterile covering over the burns until Ben can see him. I also put up a drip.'

'Good man.' John nodded his approval. 'You had better get Mark to see it. Ben will be tired.' Mark Simpson was the junior surgical registrar.

'Right,' Martin said, his face brightening as he reached for the phone.

John rose and stretched his arms above his head. 'I'm for bed,' he said.

The nurses left the office with him. 'I'm having my tea first,' Martin said in an aggrieved voice.

'Well, pour some for Winnie as well,' Laura said, seeing Winnie pull a face.

The department was quiet and Laura was in the office, wondering how Lydia was, when Ben appeared at three o'clock. 'How about a cup of tea?' he asked wearily, sinking into a chair.

'Sure. Go to the staff-room. I'll just tell Sally where we are.' She couldn't refuse him, for he looked so tired.

Laura found him sprawled in one of the armchairs,

his long legs stretched out before him, his ankles crossed. His eyes were closed in a drawn face, but they opened when he heard her shut the door.

She filled the kettle and plugged it in. 'How's Mrs Grover?' she asked as she put two teabags into the pot.

Ben took a deep breath, then let it out, as he hauled himself up in the chair. 'I don't know,' he said, frowning. 'When we opened her up, we found a badly damaged chunk of her intestines. I ressected it, but the contents had already spilled into the peritoneum.' He shrugged. 'We washed it out as well as we could, but there's bound to be infection.' His shoulders drooped. 'She lost a lot of blood and we're replacing it as fast as we can and giving her massive doses of antibiotics. She has a tube down and we're aspirating the stomach contents. So far there's no faecal matter in it, so cross your fingers.'

Laura hid her surprise at hearing the doubt in his voice. He had always been so positive—always been so right. She wanted to go to him and kiss his worries away. Instead, she made the tea and passed him a mug with the sugar bowl. 'I don't take it,' he said, gesturing towards the sugar.

Laura knew this, but, 'It's supposed to help in cases of shock,' she said quietly.

'Did you think I must be suffering from shock because I sound doubtful?' he asked, raising an eyebrow.

His black hair was awry, where he had snatched off his operation cap, and his shirt was open at the neck; Laura could see the tip of his tie peeping from his pocket. She had never seen him in such disarray. He was always so immaculate.

'No, of course not,' she said, a little too quickly, more so because she had an insane desire to run her fingers through his hair to straighten it, to kiss the soft part of his neck where it showed below his Adam's apple.

Ben sipped his tea without the sugar. 'Finding out things about me you didn't know?' he asked with a touch of sarcasm.

'Perhaps,' she answered honestly.

'I told you before, things aren't always what they seem.' He finished his tea.

Laura frowned.

Tiredness, coupled with anxiety over his patient and frustration because he was held by his Hippocratic oath, made him blurt out, 'Did you ever think that I *wasn't* to blame for David not having chemotherapy?' He leapt to his feet, caught hold of the top of her arms and said, 'Did you ever think that, just once?'

Shock held her speechless. Ben pushed her roughly aside so that she nearly fell. 'No, of course not.' His face was grim.

He flung himself out of the office, leaving Laura rubbing her arms and wondering what he meant.

CHAPTER EIGHT

THROUGHOUT her three weeks on night duty, Laura puzzled over Ben's words. She did not see him to talk to during this time. She thought he must be avoiding her and she was glad. What had he meant by saying that he was not responsible for David not having chemotherapy? Ben had been the doctor on the case.

She slept badly during the day and was tired at night. Sister Connolly was back and Sally left A and E to relieve those of the staff who had nights off in various wards.

Sally was still living at the flat, even though Laura had bought it. 'Would it be all right if I stay here while I'm on night duty?' Sally had asked Laura when the negotiations were completed. 'I know I was to move in with Geoffrey, but it's difficult enough to sleep in the day without someone coming in at lunchtime.'

'Of course you must stay,' Laura had insisted. She did not particularly want to be on her own. She needed Sally to distract her from her thoughts of Ben.

Laura wished her parents lived in Ledborough. It would have been marvellous to go home and relax. She couldn't even go to the house, for her parents had let it.

Her nights off were spent trying to catch up with

her sleep, but in this she was not too successful. Her dreams were full of David interspersed with Ben, but it was Ben's arms she longed to feel about her when she awoke.

What had he meant when he'd said, 'Did you ever think that I *wasn't* to blame?' Surely he didn't mean that she was?

Tormented and puzzled, she lost weight, and was so nervous that the slightest noise made her jump. 'What you need is a holiday,' Sally told her. 'Why don't you go and see your parents on your nights off?'

'It's too far for four days,' Laura told her. She couldn't tell her friend that she didn't want to leave Ledborough, not when there was a chance of catching a glimpse of Ben when she came off duty in the morning.

It was on the last night of her night duty that she almost bumped into him. She was just coming on duty, feeling weary, and met him coming out of the emergency resuscitation room.

The unexpectedness of their encounter sent her blood racing and desire flaring. All those dreams were as nothing when confronted with the real thing. He was all man, big and strong. She could see her desire reflected in his eyes. It was impossible to hide the strong attraction they had for each other.

She wanted to question him about David's treatment, but her mouth was too dry. All she could do was stand and look at him, drown in his brown eyes.

Ben had deliberately avoided seeing Laura, so seeing her unexpectedly—he had thought her night duty was over—caught him as defenceless as she was, and as unable to hide his desire for her as she was to hide hers from him.

'I've just been to see a patient,' he said, thinking that it sounded as if he was making an excuse for being there.

Laura ran her tongue over her dry lips. Seeing the pink, moist tip roused Ben even further. 'What happened?' she managed to ask, hoping her voice didn't sound as hoarse to him as it did to herself.

'Martin called me in.' He studied her face carefully to see her reaction at the mention of Martin's name and saw her blush. Obviously some relationship between them, he decided bleakly. Even though a relationship between himself and Laura seemed impossible, he could not still his longing for her. 'A man was thrown through a glass window in a pub fight. He has multiple cuts, some of them deep, involving muscle. I'm just going to Theatre now.'

He took a step nearer to her, holding her with his eyes; his longing for her was clear in their depths.

Laura leaned towards him, her mouth slightly parted, but the door opened behind him and the patient, a big man who overflowed the trolley, was wheeled out. Two male nurses endeavoured to restrain him as a porter pushed the trolley. The man threw off the cellular blanket that was covering him, using one arm. The other one had a drip inserted in it and it was strapped to the trolley. He was naked except for his briefs. Blood was oozing through the pressure dressings on his chest and arms, thighs and lower legs.

He was restless and abusive and would have been on the floor if the nurses hadn't restrained him. He glanced up at Ben as the trolley passed. 'What are you tying me down for?' Laura smelt the alcohol on his breath as he spoke.

'He's fighting the sedative,' Ben said, glancing at Laura. 'Any other man less strong would have been out for the count by now.' He indicated for the porter to stop and stepped forward. 'This is a hospital,' he told the man firmly. 'We don't need this row. It's not helping either you or us. If you continue to fight like this, you'll die from loss of blood.' He spoke bluntly as he leaned closer to the man. 'Do you understand me?' he asked him, his words clipped and distinct.

The man, Richard Greggs, a forty-year-old with thick red hair, glared belligerently at Ben. 'All right, all right,' he said irritably.

'Thanks, Mr Kendricks,' the male nurse said, and they moved off.

Laura thought Ben would follow the trolley and made to move away, but he put a hand on her arm and said, 'Mrs Grover's holding her own.'

'Yes.' She slipped her arm from his grasp, not because she didn't want to feel his touch, but because she wanted his touch too much. 'I know, I asked.'

'Must go,' Ben said wearily. 'The theatre will be wondering what's happened to me.' And he left her.

There was a kind of grief in the bereavement his departure left her with. She sighed and went to report for duty.

Night duty had meant that Laura had so far missed the usual rush of children with cuts, sprains and broken limbs that came to Accident and Emergency during the school holidays.

'Ah, Staff,' said Linda Connolly, the night sister, a cheerful woman of thirty who had to watch her diet. 'Just in time to go with Russell.' She beamed at Laura, who had not seen Martin as he was bending down to retrieve his pen from behind the desk. 'A boy of fourteen, Edward Ritchie, has been brought in. He fell out of a tree. I've put him into cubicle three. Looks as if he's fractured his heel. He has a collar on in case there are any spinal injuries.'

'How does Linda know the boy's fractured his heel?' Martin said in a disgruntled way as he left the office with Laura. 'She's not a doctor.'

'Probably because she's had quite a few years' experience in A and E,' Laura said drily.

Martin reddened. 'Huh!'

The boy was big for his age, the same height as Laura, who was five foot six. One of his pals was sitting beside him. 'Don't tell his dad, will you?' the youth—he was more than a boy—asked anxiously. 'He'll leather him if you do.'

'Just wait outside,' Laura said with a reassuring smile.

'Well?' Martin barked the word. 'How did you come to do this? You should be home at this hour.'

The boy's face stiffened. 'The nights are still light, and how d'you think I did it?' he asked insolently.

He would be a handsome man when he grew to adulthood and lost his puppy fat, but the hardness in his eyes would detract from his looks. What had made him like that? wondered Laura, feeling compassion for the youth.

'You got run over by a big mouth,' Martin said sarcastically, glaring at Edward.

The youth's look of astonishment was replaced by a laugh, and then he winced with pain. His expression became more like a child's as he said, 'I fell out of a tree.'

'And landed on your heels rather than your head. A pity,' Martin said. 'It might have cracked some sense into it.'

Laura was quite impressed by Martin's diagnosis. She did not have much confidence in him as a doctor, unlike her unreserved admiration for Ben's skill. She was also surprised at his sarcastic quips. He had never shown any sign of a sense of humour, even a black one.

'OK, Edward,' Martin continued. 'We'll X-ray you to make sure you haven't any other fractures.'

'It's Eddie,' the boy said reluctantly. 'Is that what this is for, and why I was told not to move?' Eddie touched the collar. 'I've seen it on telly.'

'Yes,' Martin said, examining Eddie's heels. His socks and trainers had already been removed. 'Looks as if you've fractured your calcaneum and maybe your tibia. It's difficult to say until we can examine you properly, and we can't do that until the X-ray tells us that you haven't any back injuries,' Martin said.

'What's a cal—cal?' Eddie asked.

'Your heel-bone,' Martin explained, without the usual show of impatience Laura was accustomed to find in him.

'And a tib——?'

'The tibia is this bone.' Martin touched the front

of Eddie's leg below the knee. 'The bone beside it is called the fibula.'

'If I've broken my heel, what makes you think I might have injured my back?' Eddie asked. 'I landed on my feet.'

Laura wanted to know why as well, and waited for Martin's reply with interest. 'Landing on your heels can transmit a shockwave that can injure other bones—leg, back-bone, even the skull.' Martin tapped Eddie's head.

He turned to Laura. 'We'll need to give him some pethidine for the pain.' That Eddie had pain was obvious from the paleness of his face, the perspiration on his forehead and upper lip and the way he clenched his hands. He was trying not to show it.

'However, you seem to have been lucky.' Martin smiled, something else that Laura saw him seldom do with the patients. 'Staff will be back in a minute. She'll give you something for the pain as soon as your parents come. Sister's informed them. Then you'll go to X-ray.'

Eddie's face became bleak. 'You'll be lucky to find them,' he said. 'They'll be at the pub.'

'Ah.' Martin looked at Laura.

'Do you have any brothers and sisters?' Laura asked, wondering if he had, and if a babysitter was looking after them.

'A brother and a sister, younger than me.'

'Who's looking after them?' Laura asked.

'Gran,' Eddie told her.

The worry lines left Laura's face. 'Well, she can give permission for your injection,' she said.

'I thought you only had to have permission for an

operation,' Eddie said. Then, seeing Laura's look of surprise at his knowing this, added smugly, 'My little brother had his tonsils out.' Then his face became apprehensive. 'Will I have to have an operation?' he asked.

'No, we'll just put a padding of wool from your toes to your knee and bandage it with a elastic-type bandage called a crêpe bandage,' Martin told him. 'We'll keep you in for the night. And, to answer your other question, we're not allowed to give injections to a patient under the age of sixteen without a parent's consent.'

'Could I be a doctor?' Eddie asked.

'You certainly could,' Martin said. 'But you have to work hard at school to get good A levels and plenty of them, including the sciences.'

'Oh, that's no problem,' Eddie said with confidence.

'Well, then. Don't fall out of any more trees!'

They all laughed.

Laura went with Martin back to the office.

'Eddie's grandmother's contacted his parents. The father's coming in,' Linda Connolly informed them.

'Oh.' Laura looked apprehensive.

'Something wrong?'Sister asked.

'Just that Eddie's friend mentioned the father would give Eddie a beating.'

Sister's face became stern. 'Not in this hospital, he won't.'

Martin sat and started on the paperwork and Laura went to the waiting area to take the next patient. She had to call Martin back to see the patient, who had a septic finger.

'I work nights in the printing-room of the *Ledborough Daily News*,' the man, George Teller, explained. 'I thought it was just a bit red, but when I went to work it started to throb and my boss sent me here.'

The finger was red, and swollen at the end by the nail with a small amount of pus exuding from it. Martin took a look and said, 'Are you allergic to penicillin?'

George shook his head. 'No.'

'We'll give you antibiotic tablets to take home with you. Go to your doctor tomorrow.' He turned to Laura. 'Just the usual dressing.' Laura knew he meant a dressing of magnesium sulphate to draw the pus. 'I'll write him up in the office.'

Laura dressed the finger, then returned to the office for the antibiotic. Martin had just finished writing up the notes. 'Linda left the tablets for you,' he said, indicating a bottle lying on the desk. 'Eddie's father has been and Linda is giving the pethidine.'

'Was there any trouble?' Laura asked.

'No. He'd had a drink or two, I'd say, but he wasn't belligerent. Said he'd tell his son off, though. Even apologised for Eddie falling out of the tree and giving us work.'

'You seem to be very interested in Eddie's case,' Laura said as she picked up the bottle, labelled with the dose to take.

'Yes,' Martin said enthusiastically. 'I think I'll specialise in orthopaedics when my six months is up here.'

Laura gave him a big smile. She was delighted to

hear this. She had wondered at one time if Martin had chosen the wrong profession. Just shows how wrong you can be, she thought, and Ben's words, 'Did you ever think that I *wasn't* to blame?' leapt into her mind, disturbing her afresh.

Ben entered the office. He had come back especially to see Laura. There must be some way they could. . . Then he saw the smile she was giving Martin, and seeing the gentleness of it made him think that he was too late. Martin was nearer Laura's age, so it would be natural for her to find his company more conducive than his, and Martin did not have the drawback of having supposedly failed her husband. Now I'll have to think of some excuse for being here, he thought irritably.

Laura, seeing the bleakness of his expression, thought something must have happened in Theatre to upset him, and said, 'Everything all right with the patient?'

'Yes. We stitched him up and—er. . .'

Sister came in just then, saving him from having to make some banal excuse. 'Leave something?' she asked.

'Is my stethoscope here?' It wasn't. It was in his office, as he very well knew.

'I don't think so.' Sister looked at Laura. 'Have you seen it?'

'No, but I'll have a look for it when I've given Mr Teller his tablets.'

Sister nodded. Laura heard her ask Ben if he would like some coffee, and his reply in the affirmative as she left the office.

Laura had just handed over the bottle and

explained the dosage, and was about to leave when Martin parted the cubicle curtains. 'I've written to your doctor, Mr Teller,' he said, handing the patient an envelope. 'Make an appointment to see him tomorrow and give it to him. You'll need to have your finger re-dressed, anyway.'

'Thanks, Doctor,' George said.

Martin accompanied Laura on her search for Ben's stethoscope. There was no trace of it.

'What about coming out to dinner with me tomorrow?' he asked.

'Thanks for asking,' Laura said, 'but I plan to spend my nights off in bed.' She felt more kindly disposed towards Martin now that she had realised he was serious about medicine, but did not want to encourage him socially.

'I'll call for you next Saturday, then.'

For a moment she had to think what he meant, then she remembered the ball. 'Fine. I'll be ready at half-past eight.' The ball was to start at nine.

Martin left her and she returned to the office. 'Sorry, no stethoscope,' she told Ben. 'You must have left it somewhere else.'

'Thanks for looking.' He rose to his feet, thanked Linda for the coffee and left the office at the same time as Laura, who was going to change the disposable sheet on the bed in the cubicle she had just left.

'Going to the ball?' he asked impersonally, drawn into following her into the cubicle.

'Yes.'

The confines of the cubicle seemed to draw them closer, so that her awareness of him became so great that nothing existed but him. Her eyes burned with a longing she could not hide, and Ben saw it.

'Ben,' she whispered, taking a step closer to him.

She was in his arms, his mouth coming down upon hers in a passionate kiss that left her breathless. 'Oh, Ben, Ben.'

'Laura, my darling. Laura——' His voice broke as he spoke her name, then his lips were on hers again. His arms tightened about her and passion flared intensely between them, so that she forgot how she had blamed Ben for not prolonging her husband's life. She forgot everything except that she was in his arms.

When they finally broke apart, breathing heavily, she said, with her lips close to his, 'I've been sleeping, eating and thinking of you all the time.' The tears were running down her face.

'I must see you.' His voice was husky with passion as he gently wiped her tears away with his finger. 'I want you.' His voice was tense. 'I can't wait any longer. It's been torment ever since we kissed.'

'I know, Ben, darling. I know,' she whispered, trembling with longing.

'When, then?' The urgency in his tone was unmistakable.

'This is my last night on duty.'

'Good.' He gave a heartfelt sigh. 'Tomorrow evening, then.' He touched the purple smudges beneath her eyes. 'After you've had a sleep to get rid of these.' His voice had softened again.

'You're to blame for those,' she told him, tracing the outline of his lips with her finger. 'I couldn't sleep properly for thinking about you.'

'I like the sound of that.' But her touch had inflamed him again and he caught her to him, kissing her urgently, deeply. It was the noise of a trolley's wheels passing the cubicle that brought them back to where they were. 'See you tomorrow evening,' he said huskily, loath to let her go, and she, her arms about him, clung to him. 'I'll pick you up at the flat at seven.'

Laura pouted. 'So late?'

'You should be able to sleep tomorrow, and you need it.' He pretended to be stern.

'Very well, Doctor,' she said with a grin. 'I'll take your prescription.'

She watched him stride away, knowing he would look back at her from the door. He did, blowing her a kiss, not caring who saw.

CHAPTER NINE

LAURA didn't think she would be able to sleep for excitement when she came off duty at eight o'clock next morning. She was glad Sally was on nights off and staying at Geoffrey's, for her friend would have been sure to comment at the change in her. After setting her alarm for six, she went to bed.

When she awoke, stretching, she lay in the bed's warmth with a sense of anticipation. Turning on her side, she pulled one of the pillows from beneath her head and hugged it to her.

It was soft, unlike Ben's muscular body. Thoughts of being made love to by him inflamed her skin and filled her with frustration.

She tossed back the bedclothes and hurried to the shower, setting it to run cold after soaping, to cool her hot skin—hot more from her thoughts than the water. Gasping with the shock, she turned it off, stepped out and dried herself, feeling vibrantly alive.

She made herself a cup of coffee and took it to the bedroom. As Laura pondered on what to wear she applied a light make-up, with just a touch of pink lipstick, brushed her wavy hair until it shone, and wondered afresh if she should tint it a lighter colour. She had never liked the light brown it was.

She chose a black linen-type dress, with no collar and short sleeves, recently bought. It was double-breasted, simple and smart, the sort of dress that would be acceptable no matter where they went. She teamed it with black suede shoes and bag, and debated about a jacket. The weather was not particularly warm, so she took a white jacket of a heavy crêpe material from the wardrobe and put it on.

Looking at herself in the mirror, she was glad she had not worn the black jacket that matched the dress. The white lifted the dark colour, otherwise she would have looked as if she was in mourning.

Thinking of mourning brought David's face, reflected into the mirror beside her own, but it was not accompanied by the guilt that she seemed to have lived with ever since she had first met Ben. At last she was free of doubt, and she felt as if a great load had been lifted from her.

The bell rang at that moment and, knowing it was Ben, excitement gripped her. David no longer looked back at her from the mirror; it was Ben who was reflected there.

She wanted to fly to the door, but made herself walk. With each step she took her heart beat faster as her excitement increased.

Ben looked even bigger, dressed as he was in a dark grey suit, his white shirt emphasising his tanned face. A tie of muted grey, silver and blue completed his outfit. He was devastatingly attractive. His brown eyes lit with something more than admiration when he saw her. There was the anticipation she was feeling lying in their depths.

'I'd suggest staying here,' he said, his voice husky with desire. 'But I think a meal as part of the ritual would. . .'

'Make the dessert even more enticing?' she finished for him, her voice unintentionally low and alluring.

'Very well put,' he said with an amused smile, as his eyes held hers. It was as if he had caressed her.

In the car, Laura deliberately introduced their work, hoping that talking about a patient would help to compose her and still the trembling of her limbs. 'Has Rose decided on adoption?' she asked.

He gave her a quick glance, before concentrating on the road again. 'Yes, she has. She's a very brave young lady.'

He turned into the High Street and soon they had reached the five-star Ledborough Hotel.

'The only stipulation she made was that they would tell him about her when he was older and let him contact her if he wanted to.' He switched off the engine and turned to look at Laura. 'She didn't want him having to search for her, as so many adoptive children do when they grow up.'

'What a remarkable girl,' Laura said admiringly.

'Yes. She also decided to move away and plans to apply to a hospital in another city for her nurse's training.'

They were shown a table in the dining-room. It reminded her of the park's Pavilion café, with its panelled walls and white damask tablecloths. But the quality here was far superior. The place-settings were solid silver and the glasses cut-glass, their rainbow colours shining in the electric light.

Starting on their garlic mushrooms, they did not speak. They didn't need to, for their eyes did all the talking for them, but by the end of the first course they were laughing.

'Do you know that garlic is an aphrodisiac?' Ben asked in a seductive voice.

'Yes,' Laura whispered, held by the intensity of his eyes until she felt she would drown in them.

'But we don't need any help, do we?' Ben asked, his eyes darkening with desire.

'No,' she whispered, and took a gulp of her wine.

The passion that lay beneath their calmness showed in their sudden lack of appetite, causing them to eat sparingly of the steak which came next. The waiter asked anxiously, 'Is the meal to your liking?' as he took away their plates.

'Yes. It's superb,' Ben told him. 'But we shouldn't have had the mushrooms.' His eyes were smiling and Laura laughed.

Each mouthful they took seemed to increase their tension.

'I don't think we'll stay for coffee, do you?' Ben asked, reaching for her hand.

'No. Let's go.' Her voice whispered from dry lips.

He helped her on with her jacket and left his hands on her shoulders for a moment or two. She could feel them tremble, and twisted her head round to look up at him. The desire she saw in his darkened eyes set her heart racing. He kissed her lightly on the lips and she leant her cheek upon his hand. It didn't matter that they were in the entrance hall of the hotel. Nothing mattered except their desire for each other.

Ben saw her into the passenger seat of the car, pulling the seatbelt across her chest for her, his hand brushing upon the material of her dress. She had to clamp her lips hard together to prevent herself crying out, her nerve-endings were so taut.

There was an urgency about the way he drove, spurting to catch the traffic lights. Was he taking her to the flat? Laura wondered. But no. It was into Rosemary Gardens he turned the car, and then into his own drive.

As he helped her out he said, 'I thought you would prefer to come here rather than your flat. I know how you like this house.'

Laura was delighted. 'It's almost like coming home,' she said, hugging his arm as they approached the front door, and then felt embarrassed. Would he think she was hinting?

'I suppose there is a resemblance to your old home,' he said, letting her in.

'Yes,' Laura agreed, thankful that her suspicion was unfounded.

'Would you like a drink?' he asked as he helped her off with her jacket.

When she didn't answer, unable to do so because standing in the confines of the hall so close to him had roused her desire to fever-pitch, he turned from hanging her jacket on the hall-stand and pulled her into his arms.

Before his lips came down upon hers, he looked deep into her eyes and she into his. What she saw there was reflected in her own. A relief that now they could at last quench that unbearable yearning that had plagued them both for so long.

His kiss became deeper and more insistent as she responded with an abandonment she had not known she was capable of. They were both trembling as they broke apart. 'Laura,' he murmured, his lips close to hers.

She was so overcome by emotion that she could only look at him lovingly; speech was impossible.

Ben swept her up into his arms and carried her up the stairs to his bedroom. It would be only after they had made love that she would see how the room reflected his personality. The furniture was mahogany, strong and sturdy—just like Ben. The wallpaper was light beige, the curtains were patterned in navy and beige that matched the duvet cover and the carpet was plain, dark blue. The décor was dramatic and yet calming—just like Ben.

He stood her on her feet and she staggered a little as he drew the curtains. Then he came back to her, and with each step that he took her heart beat a little faster.

She was not shy with him as she had been with David. Laura revelled in Ben's touch, a touch that opened a door she had not known was there. Each caress roused her to an excited pitch that shot her into a burst of sunlight that became brighter as he took her slowly and skilfully to the peak of their lovemaking.

She did not think how David's lovemaking had been gentle and controlled out of consideration for her, and how it had restrained her, or that she had not liked to hurt his feelings by telling him so, for Ben filled her whole horizon to the exclusion of everything else.

With Ben she was released, and could allow herself to flower, each petal he opened a revelation to her.

They made love again and again, and each time their passion rose even higher, so that eventually they lay exhausted in each other's arms.

'I didn't know it could be like this,' she whispered, and immediately felt as if she had betrayed David somehow, and buried her face in Ben's shoulder.

Ben's arm tightened about her. 'I know David made you very happy and fulfilled,' he whispered. 'But you are mature now——' he gave a small laugh '——and probably sex-starved.'

She gave him a playful punch, only too eager to believe what he was saying.

In the early morning, as the birds started to sing, they showered and soaped each other playfully. But as they rubbed each other dry, holding each other with their eyes, their passion rose and they returned to the still warm bed, to glory in each other once more.

Eventually they slept, with their arms about each other. The alarm's ring woke them.

Ben groaned. 'I wish I was on night duty,' he said, slipping out of bed.

Laura moved over to his side, pulling the duvet up to her chin, wrapping his warmth about her. 'I wish you were, too.' She smiled up at him mischievously as he stood naked at the side of the bed, a powerful, beautiful figure of a man.

Ben laughed. 'You cheeky creature.' He bent to kiss her and she captured his face in her hands, holding him until he slipped down on the bed beside her. 'Darling, I don't want to go,' he whispered huskily.

'I know, and it wasn't fair of me keep you.' Her eyes were luminous with love, but she released him and sat up in bed. 'I'll be here when you come back.'

Ben's face brightened. 'I'd like that very much.'

As he showered, Laura snuggled down in the bed, hugging the duvet about her. When he returned to the bedroom she watched every movement he made. The way he put his right leg into his briefs; the way he slipped his shirt on, then his trousers and socks. He was impressive when dressed, though Laura decided that she preferred him without clothes and blushed.

She liked the way he knotted his tie in a small knot. She had never liked the big knots some men affected.

'I should have cleaned your shoes for you,' she said suddenly, moving to slip out of bed. 'And I must make your breakfast.'

His hand pushed her back on to the pillow. 'Not today,' he said with a smile. 'You need the rest.' He studied her pale face, noting its thinness. 'I'll bring you breakfast in bed.'

'Will you do this every morning?' she asked, smiling up at him.

'We'll discuss that later,' he said in a jokey way as he left her, and, too happy in herself, she didn't see the thoughtfulness in his eyes.

'Hmm.' Laura slipped under the duvet again, gloating in the feeling of completeness that she had never experienced before.

She was nearly asleep when he returned with a tray of bacon and eggs, toast, marmalade and tea. Used to having only coffee and toast, she doubted that she would be able to eat such a full breakfast, but didn't tell Ben.

Laura smiled as she took the tray from him. 'Marvellous,' she said.

'Eat every bit of it,' he instructed, bending to give her a kiss. 'You must keep up your strength.

'Indeed, I must,' she said, giving him an alluring look.

He took the tray from her and put it on the floor. 'You shameless creature,' he said, his voice rough with desire as he pulled her into his arms and kissed her.

It took a tremendous effort for him to put her aside. 'Must go,' he whispered. Ben put the tray back on her lap.

'Bye,' whispered Laura with a sigh, as the door closed behind him.

She started to eat and, much to her surprise, finished not only the bacon and eggs but the toast and marmalade as well.

Setting the tray on the floor, she lay down again, and closed her eyes and slept. She was shocked to find it was four o'clock when she woke.

Slipping out of bed, she went and showered, singing as the water cascaded over her, feeling more alive than she had ever felt in her life.

The clothes she had worn for their dinner were not appropriate for the day, so she decided to return to her flat and change.

She washed the dishes, made the bed with fresh linen, vaccumed the carpet and dusted the house. As she did so, she wondered if Ben would ask her to marry him. Was that what he had meant when he had said 'We'll discuss that later,' in answer to her query as to whether he would bring her breakfast in bed every day?

The thought that she might live with Ben in this house that she loved so much filled her with joy, a joy she quickly suppressed. He hadn't said he loved her, just as she hadn't confessed her love for him. He didn't own the house. So stop day-dreaming, she told herself.

On her way home, Laura bought some food for their evening meal. She decided to have garlic bread as a starter, with a side salad, then goulash on rice with baby sweetcorn, tiny carrots and peas. The sweet would be a fresh fruit salad of peaches, pears, strawberries, pineapple and apricots with fresh cream. A cheese-board with biscuits would follow and, to finish, coffee with mints. Her mouth watered at the prospect.

Loaded with her goods, she managed to stop at a wine shop and collect a bottle of white and red to go with the meal.

Once in her flat, she changed into jeans, a blue-and white-striped T-shirt and flat shoes. Deciding that it would be better to prepare the meal in a kitchen she was familiar with, she set to work.

She had left Ben's house at half-past four. By the time she had cooked the goulash and prepared the rest of her dinner it was six o'clock. She would ring Ben and suggest that they had their meal here to save having to reheat it when she returned to Rosemary Gardens.

It would be better if she changed before she

phoned him, Laura thought, and slipped on a simple though smart blue linen dress.

She was just putting some lipstick on when the bell went. Wondering who it could be—perhaps Sally wanted something?—she opened the door.

Surprise at seeing Ben stiffened her face for a moment, and she was just going to tell him that she had been about to phone him when he said, 'What are you doing here?' his tone sharp with disappointment. He had seen the stiffening of her face and had thought she was regretting their night of love.

'I came home to change,' she said, shock at his tone making her voice sharp. 'I'd bought something for our evening meal and decided to cook it here, and then, rather than carry it to your house and reheat it, I was going to suggest we have dinner here.' Sudden tears moistened her eyes. 'I was just about to phone you.'

'Laura, darling. I'm so sorry.' Ben stepped into the flat and took her into his arms. 'It's just that I had a fright when I came home and found you not there.'

Laura could feel his heart beating quickly beneath the hand she had placed on his chest.

'I thought you were regretting last night,' he told her.

She looked up into his face and saw traces of fear still in his eyes. He loves me, she thought in wonderment, and her face lit with joy. 'I love you, Ben,' she whispered. 'I will never leave you.' As she spoke these last words she felt a tremor of fear, but decided it was just the natural fear associated with losing a loved one.

'And I you, Laura, my darling.' He kissed her with a kiss that almost bruised her lips, putting all his fear at the thought that he had lost her into that kiss.

Laura responded passionately.

The dinner was forgotten as passion took hold of them. She didn't remember their going into the bedroom, she was so overwhelmed with love. Their lovemaking was different from how it had been last night. It was frantic, mainly because he had thought he had lost her.

And Laura, although she had thought she had dismissed her fear, responded in the same way. They behaved as a couple who had found each other alive after being parted in an accident or shipwreck. They couldn't have enough of each other.

Endearments fell from their lips—'Laura, my darling'—'Ben, my dearest'—and even when they lay exhausted they held each other close.

Eventually, they rose and showered. 'Did you say something about dinner?' Ben asked as he watched her brush her hair. It was a dark day and the electric light caught fair highlights in the strands.

'Oooh, yes.' She twisted round to look at him in horror, then her face relaxed. 'Oh, thank goodness. I hadn't put it in,' she remembered.

They were both hungry, and ate every bit of their dinner. The sexual tension was gone so they could enjoy their meal and discover how hungry they were.

'I didn't know you were such a good cook,' Ben said, giving a sigh of satisfaction as he took the last mouthful of his sweet.

Laura was about to say, Oh, yes, you did. Don't

you remember coming to dinner with David and I? and just stopped herself. It was not because guilt and doubts had risen again, especially about not having loved her husband. She knew she had loved David, as she knew, now, that it had only been the confusion of her feelings for Ben that had caused her to think that she had *not* loved him. It was because she felt it would have been an insensitive thing to say.

Following their meal, they sat side by side on the couch, arms about each other. 'So when will you marry me?' Ben asked.

Laura looked up at him and saw how the angles of his face had softened. 'As soon as possible,' she said quickly, with a smile.

'I have some leave due me, but I won't be able to take it for another month,' he told her. 'If I took it earlier it would mean putting back the lists, and they're long enough already.' He bent to kiss her lips. 'The patients will have to come first, I'm afraid, my darling.'

'Next time I fall in love, I'll make it a bank manager,' Laura teased.

'There's not going to be a next time,' Ben told her. 'This is for good.'

Laura kissed him, so that he wouldn't see the sadness that had entered her eyes. She had thought when she married David that it would be for life, and it hadn't been.

Ben sensed what she was trying to hide. 'We're not going to die,' he said. 'We're going to live to a ripe old age and drive our children mad. Then we'll just fade away together, like leaves that fall from a tree.'

He looked rather solemn, so she said, 'I didn't know you were poetic,' to lighten their mood.

'There's a lot you have to learn about me,' he said. 'I hope you won't be disappointed.'

'So do I,' she jested.

'You cheeky madam.' He grinned down at her, and then the grin left his face as his love for her engulfed him. 'Oh, Laura,' he said softly, and kissed her. Lifting his lips from hers, he wrapped his arms about her, holding her close to his heart. 'I never want to let you go,' he said, so quietly she had to strain to hear him.

Suddenly, the responsibility of being loved so intensely almost overwhelmed Laura. David's love had not been like this. It had been undemanding. Ben's love would demand everything: her body and her mind. Willingly she would give it all to him, for she loved him so deeply that it frightened her.

They did not discuss when they would marry. Arrangements for that would be made when they could think of something other than the overwhelming desire to be in each other's arms, to feel their bodies close to each other, to show each other how much they loved each other by expressing it physically.

At breakfast next morning Ben said, 'Much as I would like us to live together, I think that we'll have to wait until we're married.' He reached for her hand across the breakfast table, knocking the marmalade pot over. It lay where it had fallen as he said, 'Both of us working at the hospital would create gossip.'

He gave her hand a squeeze. 'One thing you can be sure of is that it would be on the hospital grapevine before you had emptied your suitcase at my house.' He frowned slightly. 'I am right in thinking you want to live at Rosemary Gardens?'

She smiled at his assumption. 'Yes. I would like to, very much.'

'It's a pity I can't take you to the dance, but I've asked Bea.' He leaned forward and kissed her. 'Never mind. We can still have most of the dances.'

'I don't think Bea will like that.'

'No, I don't suppose so, but she'll just have to.' He kissed her again. 'Next year we'll be together.'

'Yes,' she said, with love in her eyes.

But as she closed the door, after he had gone, she felt a shiver of apprehension. Dismissing it with an impatient shrug, she went back into the flat to wash the dishes.

CHAPTER TEN

THEIR duties kept them separated more than they would have wished over the next few days. Laura was on the late shift, which meant that by the time she was off duty it was at least ten-thirty before she arrived home, and Ben's Theatre work was heavy. They were both tired when they did manage to meet.

The evening of the dance, Laura slipped on a gown she had bought especially for Ben. It was black, with a boat neckline and puffed sleeves, and fitted at the waist with a full skirt. Roses of the same material nestled at the bottom of the sleeves and the waist. A bow at the back completed the dress. It was lined with a net underskirt.

She had been sure of the dress when she had tried it on in the shop, but had had doubts when she had arrived home, and put it on now with some trepidation. As she swirled in front of the mirror, Laura smiled. She looked good. The black made her skin appear creamy.

She had let her hair grow, and for this occasion had had it curled and pulled back at the side of her face, to fall in tiny curls to below her neckline at the back. A couple of curls had been teased to hang at either side of her face and small curls fell on to her forehead. Silver earrings were the only jewellery she wore.

A small velvet cape went with the dress. Black

suede shoes and bag completed the outfit. She decided that a light make-up with a touch of lipstick was all she needed, for the knowledge that she was loved had lent a glow to her skin and a sparkle to her eyes.

The admiration on Martin's face and his 'Wow' when she opened the door to him at half-past eight confirmed this. If Martin reacted like this, what would Ben's reaction be? Laura wondered, and smiled more invitingly than she would normally have done.

Before she could stop him he had stepped inside, and his arms were around her, his wet lips pressed to hers. Laura pushed him away, but his grip tightened, so she stamped on his toes. This made him release her. 'Ow!' he howled as he stepped back, affronted.

'I didn't say you could kiss me,' Laura said angrily.

'I thought having to ask to kiss a girl went out in Victorian times,' he said, rubbing his foot against his other leg. 'You certainly invited it.'

Perhaps she had. She couldn't very well tell him that she had been thinking of Ben when she saw Martin's expression of admiration, could she? 'Well, I didn't mean to,' she said firmly as she collected her cape and bag. She should really have repaired her lipstick, but didn't want to keep Martin in the flat longer than was necessary.

Martin's car was a Mini and Laura's dress was crushed. Perhaps the creases will fall out, she thought, hoping the poor start to the evening was not a bad omen.

'How's that boy with the fractured heel?' she

asked, thinking that by talking shop she would defuse Martin's ardour.

'He's fine. The X-rays showed that the fractured heel was the only injury. His skull and spine were fine.' Martin paused to pass a parked car. 'I spoke to Eddie's father about his decision to take up medicine, and he was so impressed it improved the relationship between them.'

'That's great,' Laura said. 'Do you think Eddie will stick to his decision?'

'Oh, yes.' Martin was adamant about this.

They arrived at the Ledborough Hotel at the same time as Ben and his partner, and they joined up in the foyer. The slight depression Laura was feeling was not lifted when she saw Bea's dress. It was blue, the colour of her eyes, fitted, silken, and made her look dainty but sophisticated. Laura felt like a child beside her.

Laura had not seen Ben for a couple of days— days that had been arid without him. He looked magnificent. Tall, broad, handsome, his evening dress fitted him to perfection. Without realising it, Laura leant towards him, and his hand reached for her. Their partners might not have been there.

'Good evening, Laura,' he said. Even his voice had softened, and his eyes, those melting brown eyes, smiled in admiration. 'You look very lovely this evening.'

Then he noticed her smeared lipstick and knew, immediately, what had caused it, and the smile left his eyes. Surely, if Laura loved him, she would not let another man kiss her?

Laura did not see the change in his expression,

she only saw him. All the aggravation occasioned by Martin's kiss left her. She did not care if her dress was crushed. She forgot about her slightly smeared lipstick, which she had meant to repair as soon as she arrived at the hotel. Just the sight of Ben made her feel good.

'Come on, Laura,' Martin said, unable to keep the peeved note out of his voice at seeing the look that had passed between Laura and Ben. 'If we don't hurry, the best tables will be taken.'

'You're absolutely right, Martin,' Ben agreed. Taking both the ladies' arms, he swept ahead of Martin, who hurried after them.

Laura did not want Ben to take his hand from her arm. His touch filled her with longing, a longing to be in his arms, to be close to him, to feel his lips upon hers. The band was already playing, and Laura couldn't wait for him to ask her to dance.

The paediatric consultant, Joe Carter, with his wife, Anabelle, a blonde of about forty-five, with regular features gestured for them to join them. 'Come and sit with us,' he said.

'Thanks.' Ben seated the ladies, with himself next to Bea, then Martin, then Laura, which surprised her. She thought Ben would have sat next to her.

Laura was further surprised and a little hurt when Ben extended his hand towards Bea and said, 'Let's dance.' She had expected him to take her on the floor.

'You should stop pining for that man,' Martin whispered. 'You can see he's interested in Bea.'

Was he? Laura wondered anxiously, then chided

herself. For heaven's sake, he's only asked her to dance.

'What would you like to drink?' Martin asked.

'A gin and tonic, please.'

He raised his eyebrows at that. He had never known Laura to drink gin.

As soon as he had left her, Joe asked her to dance. She accepted. At least she would be on the dance-floor near Ben.

'You know you are getting older,' Joe said, 'when everyone else looks younger.'

Laura didn't know the paediatrician very well. She only assisted him on the occasions when he came to Casualty if Sister wasn't there. He had a reputation for excellence, but was rather cold with the children.

'Do you have children?' Laura asked, really for something to say.

'A girl of twenty-two, who is married, and a. . .' He hesitated slightly before adding, 'A boy of nineteen.'

Glancing up at his face, Laura saw an expression of pain in his eyes that was quickly hidden as he narrowed them. She saw something else, perhaps a resemblance to her late husband in the shape of Joe's face. Was the boy dead? she wondered, not liking to ask.

Laura was the sort of person people confided in and Joe said, 'He dropped out of medical school and vanished.'

Suddenly Laura remembered Robert Wilson. Could he be the missing son? She would have to ask Michelle. 'Perhaps he will come home,' she said, instilling a note of hope into her voice. She dared not tell him what she suspected in case Robert was not his son.

'Oh, I don't think so.' Joe's tone was rather casual, but Laura remembered the pain she had seen in his eyes. Joe was anything but casual. He was hiding his distress behind a cool exterior. Probably does the same thing to protect himself emotionally where his patients are concerned, she thought.

'Stranger things have happened,' she said quietly.

Joe looked down at the caring face raised to his. 'I'm not very good at showing my feelings to my children,' he confessed. 'And, being a perfectionist, I tend to be too critical and think I'm right.'

'Well. . .' She didn't know what to say now.

'Well, thanks.' He gave her a smile of great sweetness.

'You shouldn't ration that,' she said, and wondered if she had gone too far when she saw him frown.

'Ration what?'

Laura grinned. 'That super smile.'

Joe laughed and looked years younger. He led her back to the table. 'Thanks again,' he said.

Martin pushed her drink towards her. Laura took a big gulp and spluttered. She didn't really like gin, but it steadied her.

Surely Ben would ask her to dance now the music had changed? But no, he returned with Bea to the table and went to get their drinks.

'Come on, Laura,' Martin said, holding out his hand, and she could hardly refuse. He was her escort, after all.

He held her too closely. His breath, tainted with

alcohol, wafted past her face. She tried to pull away, but his grip tightened. 'Look, Martin,' Laura said sharply. She was not going to fight him off all evening. 'You're my partner, not my lover.'

'Oh, but we can remedy that,' he said, nibbling her ear.

He must have had a stronger drink than she had, Laura thought, as charitably as she could, and she twisted her head away.

'May I cut in?' Ben's voice came from behind them.

As Ben was a registrar, Martin had to release Laura, but he did it reluctantly. 'Not for long, my darling,' he said, giving Laura a meaningful glance.

Ben's arms tightened about her. 'Hey,' she objected, looking up into his face with a frown. 'You're hurting me.'

'Sorry.' He relaxed his arms a little.

The smile Laura had been about to give became a grimace as she saw how grim he looked. 'What's wrong?'

He didn't answer.

It could have been because he was manoeuvring her round another couple, but she didn't think so. 'What's the matter?'

The annoyance left by Martin's antics, especially his parting words, was still with Ben, and he answered irritably, 'Wrong? What could be wrong?' His tone was sarcastic.

'That's what I'm asking you,' she said, nearly tripping him up as her feet faltered in the quickstep.

He pulled her off the floor and through a French window that led into the garden at the back of the hotel. It was floodlit so she could see his face, which was tight with anger.

'I thought you said you were in love with me,' he said, holding her by the arms and only preventing himself from shaking her by a supreme effort of will.

'I am.' She couldn't hide the hurt in her voice.

'So when you're in love you kiss other men and allow them to paw you.'

The fact that it was a statement and not a question added to Laura's anger. 'You always think you're right, don't you?' The unjust accusation made her want to hurt Ben, and she lashed out at his professional integrity. 'You thought you were right with David's treatment, didn't you? And you weren't. His life could have been prolonged if you had persuaded him.'

The thought of Martin kissing Laura and holding her had infuriated Ben, but it was this accusation that shocked him into saying, 'It was David's decision not to have chemotherapy. He wouldn't let me give it to him.'

He was almost shouting now. 'David did not want you to suffer. He knew chemotherapy would only give temporary relief to his terminal condition, and that you would be filled with false hope. He loved you too much for that.'

Ben regretted it as soon as he had said it, and would have snatched the words back if he could. He regretted it professionally, he had broken his Hippocratic oath, but he did not regret her knowing. The burden he had carried since David's death had been lifted.

Laura was stunned. Her mouth gaped. She must

have mistaken what he had said. Yes, that was it. David could not have shortened his life on her account. Of course not. 'I don't believe you,' she said, her eyes bright with anger. 'No one would deliberately make such a sacrifice.'

Ben looked steadily into her eyes. His anger was gone, only compassion remained. 'Wouldn't they?' he asked her quietly. 'Perhaps not you or I, but David. . .'

It was the compassion she saw in his eyes, coupled with the softness of his tone as he mentioned her husband, that nearly convinced her. David would have done such a thing. He would have made the ultimate sacrifice for the one he loved.

A great cry escaped her lips. 'Ohhhh! No—no.' She took a step backwards, her hand pushing towards Ben, as if to push away what he had said. Laura could not accept such a sacrifice. What sort of a life would she have now, knowing that her husband had made it? No, it could not be true.

Furious anger caught hold of her. 'I don't know why you're doing this to me,' she said, icily cold. 'I know you're passionate, and passionate people might say something to hurt if they think the person they love has betrayed them, but this is going too far. I never want to see you again.'

Lifting her skirts, she swished past him. At Reception, she asked them to call a taxi. 'One has just dropped a guest,' the receptionist told her.

Laura hurried outside. The taxi was just about to leave, and stopped for her as she flagged it down. She was grateful not to have to wait, for she couldn't face anyone now.

CHAPTER ELEVEN

LAURA continued to convince herself that she was right in thinking that Ben had told her about David to hurt her because he was jealous.

She did not answer the phone the next day, Sunday, because she was sure it must be him. She almost didn't answer the door when the bell rang at midday. It was Martin calling, 'It's me, Laura,' that made her let him in. She owed him something for deserting him last evening.

'Why didn't you answer the phone?' he asked in an aggrieved tone.

'I didn't feel like it,' she replied, unable to keep the irritation out of her voice. Then, deciding that just because she had spent a sleepless night it was unfair of her to blame Martin, she said, 'Want some coffee?'

'Thanks.' He followed her into the kitchen. 'Where did you vanish to last evening?' he asked, watching as she filled the kettle.

'I didn't feel very well,' she told him, which was near to the truth.

'You should have told me,' he said, concern showing in his eyes. 'I would have run you home.'

She looked at the boyish face with a sudden rush of affection. He really was quite a nice bloke, and didn't deserve to be used the way she had used him.

She made the coffee and pushed a mug and the

bowl of sugar towards him. 'I'm sorry.' Laura thought of adding that she hadn't wanted to spoil his evening, and that that was why she had left without telling him, but decided that she had had enough of deception. Deception? Did that mean that she subconsciously believed Ben had told the truth? No. She pushed that thought aside. It was too unpalatable.

'I was upset,' she told him as she reached for the sugar, taking two spoonfuls instead of saccharins. She needed some strength, she decided.

'Ben Kendricks,' he said, not as a question but a statement. 'I thought as much.'

Sensing his sympathy, Laura nearly blurted out Ben's confession, but something held her back. It was a matter of ethics. If it became known that Ben had broken the rule that a doctor did not divulge his patient's confidences, Ben would lose his credibility. Laura didn't want that. Though she could never see Ben again, she still loved him.

'Yes,' she said.

'Never mind. You've still a friend in me.'

Laura managed a smile. It didn't look as if she would ever manage to rid herself of Martin.

She didn't notice that he was treating her as a friend, and not as someone he was in love with.

Suddenly she was glad of his faithfulness and, leaning forward with a smile, she gave him a light kiss on the lips.

'That's better,' he said, but made no move to take her into his arms.

This time Laura did see the difference in him. 'What happened after I left?'

'Ben came back to the table without you and asked if I would take Bea home, and when I said yes he left,' he told her too casually.

'Oh—h?' Laura's eyes widened.

Martin's face reddened slightly. 'Both being deserted——' he didn't make it sound accusing '—drew us together, and we found that we had many things in common.' He smiled, and it was a shy smile that wiped away the discontented lines from his face.

'I'm glad,' Laura told him, meaning it. Much as she needed a shoulder to cry on, she didn't want to encourage Martin.

'So you don't mind?' The worry lines that had settled on his face as he told her were swept away.

'Of course not.' Laura collected the empty coffee-mugs and rose from the table to wash them. 'You were only infatuated with me, but I thought Bea was in love with Ben.'

'No. She was fond of him, but he treated her too casually.'

'Oh. I thought that that was why she disliked me?'

'No.' Martin flipped back the lock of hair that had fallen over his forehead. 'She thought you were too quick to judge. She told me about how you reacted to Timmy's bruising.'

So that was why Bea had looked at her with such disdain, not because she'd thought of her as a rival.

'I'm sorry about Ben,' he said, rising from the table and putting an arm round her. 'You're fond of him, aren't you?'

'Yes, but. . .' Laura shrugged.

'It was mean of me to tell you about Bea and I.' He took the teatowel from her, hung it up and took hold of her arms to turn her to him. 'I suppose I wanted to hurt you, to pay you back for using me.'

Laura blushed. Martin was more intuitive than she had thought. 'Was it that obvious?'

Martin nodded and let her go.

'I'm sorry,' Laura said quietly. 'I hope your relationship with Bea flourishes,' she added, seeing a new maturity in him.

'So do I.'

Laura went with him to the door and kissed him, goodbye. As soon as she had closed it the phone rang. Laura ignored it, but it persisted. Unable to stand its insistent ringing, she unplugged it, snatched up her bag and cardigan and left the flat.

It was not until she was outside that she discovered it was raining. Unwilling to return, she hurried to take shelter in the art gallery that opened on Sunday.

It was as she was looking at the postcards and books for sale that she turned and bumped into a woman who was reaching between herself and the person next to Laura for one of the postcards.

'Oh, I'm sorry,' Laura said, then her eyebrows rose in surprise. It was Michelle.

'Oh, Staff.' Michelle looked uncomfortable, and made to turn away.

Laura's hand on her arm detained her. 'You're just the person I want to see.' In her anguish, Laura had almost forgotten Joe's conversation while they were dancing. Seeing Michelle had reminded her. She didn't ask her if Robert was Joe's son, she just spoke positively and said, 'Robert's surname isn't Wilson, Michelle. It's Carter.'

'How did you know?' Shock made Michelle blurt out the truth.

'I saw his father at the dance last night and deduced Robert's identity from what Joe said.'

Michelle's face tightened. 'You didn't tell him what you suspected?'

'No. I thought I would ask you first.'

Michelle sighed deeply. 'He doesn't want to see his father,' she told Laura.

'Do you think that's right?'

'It's what Robert wants,' Michelle said defensively, and turned to go.

Laura's hold tightened on Michelle's arm. 'His father is very upset,' she said quietly.

'How do you know?' The dizzy blonde was dizzy no longer. She had grown up, and was prepared to defend the man she loved. 'Robert said his father only cared about him dropping medicine, not about what he wanted.'

'I don't think that's true,' Laura told her. 'I think he cares very much, but doesn't know how to show it.'

A dreamy look came into Michelle's eyes. 'Robert's not like that,' she said softly. 'He shows his feelings.'

'We're not all alike,' Laura said sharply. 'None of us is an open book all the time.' As soon as she had said it, she wondered how well she had known David. She had thought she knew everything about him. Had he sacrificed what remained of his life for her?

She wanted to cry—No, no no, but steeled herself

144   A MATTER OF ETHICS

to put these thoughts aside and concentrate on Michelle. 'What about his mother?' Laura asked.

'He wanted to tell his mother, but knew she would tell his father. She tells him everything.'

'She loves him and wouldn't want him to suffer.'

Worry lines creased Michelle's forehead, making her look younger. 'You think I should encourage him to phone his parents, don't you?'

'Yes.' Laura's tone was firm.

'Well, I'll see what I can do,' Michelle said. 'But I can't promise he'll see them.'

'At least ask him to phone them and tell them he's all right.' Laura released her.

'I'll do my best,' Michelle promised.

It was later in the week that Joe Carter came to Laura in Casualty. 'I believe I have you to thank for Robert contacting us,' he said, looking less careworn. 'Thanks very much. He's going to marry that little nurse with whom he's living and has decided to go to art school.'

Joe looked a bit abashed. 'It's what he really wants. I tried to persuade him otherwise, thinking that a career as an artist was not secure, but I realise, now, that I was wrong.' He gave a tired smile. 'He has to have his chance, and his work is good, so perhaps he'll succeed, and I'll do all I can to help.'

Laura smiled up at him. 'I'm so glad he contacted you.'

'Thanks again,' he said, and left her.

Laura had managed to avoid Ben, who seemed to haunt Casualty, by dodging into cubicles whenever she saw him. She did so now as she saw his figure approaching.

'Hello, Staff.' A voice she knew came from the bed. It was Tracy Warren, a young woman who kept cutting her arms superficially. She had refused counselling following the death of her twin sister three months ago in a car accident. She blamed herself, as she had been driving the car when the accident happened.

Laura had thought the cubicle was empty. Tracy must have been put in there when she was talking to Joe Carter. Strips of cotton material were wrapped around Tracy's left forearm.

'What have you been up to?' she asked kindly, knowing quite well what Tracy's problem was.

Tracy looked down at her left arm. 'Oh.' She shrugged. 'It's Terry's fault. If she hadn't died. . .' There was anger and distress in the young woman's voice, and a certain wildness.

'But you know you weren't to blame,' Laura said, putting an arm round Tracy's shoulders to calm her. 'It was foggy, you had your headlights and fog-light on and were driving carefully. It was the other driver who crashed into you, going too fast.'

Tracy's eyes remained dull and Laura knew that her words had had no effect. Tracy would not be convinced. She had slashed her arms quite a few times since the crash, but always came to the A and E department that had admitted her at the time of the accident instead of going to her own doctor.

She had refused to see a psychiatrist, determined to inflict as much punishment upon herself as she could in payment for killing her sister. 'The nurse has gone for the doctor,' she said now, lethargically.

Laura was sorry for her. Tracy was in her early twenties, and would have been a pretty woman, but grief and an inability to accept that she was not responsible for her sister's death had painted lines on her face that should not have been there.

Is that what I'm doing? Laura wondered. Not accepting Ben's confession? No, of course I'm not, she told herself vehemently.

As if thinking about him had brought him, the cubicle curtain parted and he came in. 'Ooh, this is a new doctor,' Tracy said with brittle brightness. 'I haven't seen you before.'

Ben had noticed Laura slipping into the cubicle and was determined that she should not escape him this time. 'Can I help?' he asked, noting the blood-stained strips on Tracy's arms.

'I want this doctor to look at my arm,' Tracy said. She could be petulant at times.

At that moment the nurse returned, with a dressing pack and an antibiotic-impregnated Vaseline dressing packet. 'The doctor——' Nurse Hadley was about to tell Tracy that Martin was coming, but saw Ben and blushed.

'That's all right,' Ben said. 'Tell Russell that I'll attend to this patient.' He smiled at Susan Hadley, little realising how devastating his smile was.

Susan's blush deepened. The effect on her was just as great as on Laura. Though Laura managed not to blush, her heart pounded, and she had to fight to stop her hand trembling as she took the dressing pack from Susan, who just nodded at Ben before slipping away.

Normally a doctor from the surgical team only treated patients in Casualty if they were called in to advise, or if there was a major emergency when all the doctors were needed.

Laura knew why Ben had made the offer. It was four o'clock, so he must have finished his out-patients. He wanted to talk to her. She would have to try and deflect him. She didn't want to hear what he had to say. Why? a small voice asked her. Are you afraid? Yes—yes—yes. Hysteria was rising inside her.

'Well, Staff?' Ben drew her attention.

'Yes, Doctor,' she said smartly, placing the dressing pack on the trolley, one of which was kept in each cubicle. She cut it open, removed the pack, hung up the plastic bag that was included with it for putting the dirty dressing in, pulled off the top of the pack, being careful not to touch the inside, then moved to remove the makeshift bandage.

'Ow.' Tracy pulled her left arm away as Laura lifted the end; it was sticking.

'It's all right,' Laura reassured her. 'I'll get a bowl with some disinfectant and we'll soak it off.'

Quickly she did as she had said, and within seconds the cotton material loosened. Laura washed her hands and removed the material with sterile forceps, depositing it in the disposable bag along with the forceps. She then placed a sterile towel under the arm, opened the sachet of normal saline, using forceps, poured it into the small receptacle provided in the dressing pack and bathed the area.

'Oooh, its sore,' wailed Tracy.

'It will be,' Laura said. 'It's raw.'

The arm had healed scars beside the fresh cuts and the exposed area was inflamed. Scratches made with a razor had caused many red superficial lines, and some were bleeding now.

'Have you taken her temperature?' Ben asked. His tone was not accusing.

'I haven't, but Nurse Hadley might have.'

'Yes, she did,' Tracy confirmed.

Ben lifted the notes, which had been sent from Records and left by Susan. He read them carefully, seeing that his own diagnosis of self-inflicted wounds had been confirmed. 'You'll need an antibiotic,' he said, glancing at Tracy. He noted her pallor and thinness. 'And I think it might be a good idea if we admit you for a few days, to make sure your arm clears properly.' Ben glanced at the notes again and saw that Tracy had refused counselling. He would have to see if he could do something about that.

'Will you be my doctor?' Tracy asked.

'Yes.' Ben smiled at her and, like all the other women he smiled at in that especially kind way, Tracy smiled back and said, 'Good.'

So Ben has worked his magic again, Laura thought as she dried the cleaned area and applied the antibiotic tulle, non-stick melolin dressing and a pad and bandage. Tracy had always refused, in the past, to be admitted.

'We'll start you on antibiotics when you reach the ward,' he told Tracy. 'Are you allergic to penicillin?' She shook her head. He wrote her up for augmentum. 'I'll let the ward know,' he told Laura.

'Very well, Doctor,' she said, without looking at him.

She went to fetch a wheelchair. 'You know, Terry comes to me in my dreams,' Tracy said as Laura settled her into it. 'She wants me to come to her. Says she's lonely without me.'

Laura hid her extreme alarm at hearing Tracy's words. She had hoped that she wouldn't have to see Ben, but now she would have to seek him out, to tell him how Tracy's mental condition had deteriorated.

Sally was in charge of the ward when Laura and her patient arrived. Laura gave her the notes, opening them at the page where Ben had written, 'Needs watching carefully'.

Sally gave no sign that anything was amiss and directed one of the nurses to put Tracy in the bed nearest the office.

'I'm really worried about her,' Laura said, and told Sally why, thinking that her friend would be able to tell Ben and that she could escape seeing him, but the office door opened and Ben came in before Sally could reply.

He had followed Laura to the ward especially to see her. He must convince her that he had not told her about David because he was jealous, that what he had said was true.

'Ah,' Laura said, managing to hide her longing for him behind a tight smile.

Immediately the wariness left Ben's face. He assumed his welcome was because she had realised he had spoken the truth.

He was about to smile in return when she said, 'I must tell you what Tracy said.'

So he had been wrong in his assumption. 'Oh?'

Laura saw his withdrawal and was relieved, yet at the same time saddened. 'She needs urgent psychiatric help.' Her eyes were troubled. 'Tracy told me that Terry, her dead sister, wants her to join her. She said Terry was lonely.'

'This is serious,' he said. 'I'll phone Addison and ask if he can see her immediately.' Addison was the consultant psychiatrist.

'Good,' Laura said, making to move past him.

Ben caught hold of her arm. 'I want to speak to you,' he said evenly.

If Laura had looked at him she would have seen the appeal in his eyes, but she wrenched her arm away and said, 'But I don't want to speak to you.' She did look at him then, but her words had made him angry and it was this that she saw in his eyes. 'Not ever again, except professionally.'

Ben let her go, hiding his pain behind a bleak expression. 'Now who thinks they're right?' he said mockingly.

Laura wanted to run down the corridor back to A and E, but controlled her steps. She had just entered Casualty when a harassed Martin, darting out of a cubicle, caught hold of her arm and said, 'You're just the person to help me.'

Laura didn't need to be told in what way. A child's loud crying came from the cubicle he had just vacated.

As Martin swished the curtain aside, Laura saw a child of about three, struggling on its mother's knee.

'I thought I'd picked them all up,' the young mother wailed, almost as loudly as her child. Nicola Mitchell's brown hair was tied back in a ponytail, making her look younger than her twenty-six years.

'Picked what up?' Laura asked, glancing at Martin, who shrugged.

'My necklace broke, and the small beads fell all over the place,' Nicola said in a distraught way, tears running down her face. 'I was picking them up when Peter found one, and I was just too late to stop him pushing it up his nose.'

'Try and calm yourself,' Laura said in a kind voice. 'Dr Russell will soon have it removed.'

The calmness with which she spoke reassured the mother. 'Oh, will he?' she said, looking appealingly up at Martin.

'Yes,' he said, hiding his apprehension. He was not very good with children.

Laura picked a toy engine from out of the toy-box that was part of the equipment in each cubicle. 'Hi, Peter,' she said, smiling at the boy. 'Would you like to play with this engine?'

The child had quietened a little since his mother had gained control of herself. He stretched out a hand for the toy.

'We'll wait until he's settled,' Laura told the mother. 'Then I think it would be best if you hold him on your knee while I hold his head. Doctor can then look into his nose and extract the bead.'

Laura spoke more confidently than she felt. She hoped this was what would happen, but if the bead was small it might have been pushed too high to extract. Then Peter would have to be admitted and have it removed under a general anaesthetic.

'Did you bring some of the beads to show us what size they are?' Martin asked, as Peter played with the train.

Nicola reached into her bag and brought out a tissue. She opened it and Martin picked a bead out. It was small enough to put in a child's nose, but too large to be inhaled. He replaced it and put the tissue with the beads on to the trolley.

Laura sensed Martin's relief. 'Fetch the angled forceps, please, Staff,' he instructed Laura in a quiet voice.

Laura hurried away, collected the forceps kept in a sterile solution, rinsed off the solution and placed them in a kidney dish; she also brought a dressing pack.

Peter looked up as she entered the cubicle, but Laura had kept the dish and pack behind her back so as not to alarm him. She put them on a trolley behind the child, opened the pack and spread it out. It was not a sterile procedure.

'Nurse will hold his head,' Martin said, to Nicola, still in a quiet voice, 'but you will need to keep tight hold of him. Do you think you can do that?'

'I'll try, but he's strong,' Nicola said.

As soon as her hold tightened on the child he started to struggle and scream. Martin looked up Peter's nose as best he could, using a pencil torch. 'I see it,' he said, the worry lines on his forehead smoothing out.

The curtains swished aside and Ben came in. 'Want any help?' he asked.

His appearance shocked the child into silence, but only for a moment, then he started to shriek again. Ben disappeared and came back with a tabard covered in teddy bears over his suit. I should have put one of those on, thought Laura. The tabard was an apron without sleeves, slipped over the head, tied at the side, and patterned with nursery characters or teddy bears. They were worn when treating children who might be afraid of white coats.

The child quietened, intrigued by the tabard's design. 'Come and sit on my knee,' Ben said with a smile, reaching for Peter. 'Then we can count the teddies together.'

Peter stopped crying, and Ben took him from his mother and sat beside her. 'One, two, three,' Ben started to count, glancing up at Martin and Laura and giving them a nod.

Laura stepped behind him and waited for Ben to signal again. 'Peter,' Ben said as the child quietened. 'Do you think one of these teddies has a bead in his nose?' He touched the picture on his tabard.

Peter nodded. Laura turned to the toy-box in the corner behind her and picked out a teddy, intuitively guessing what Ben was trying to do. She passed it to Ben.

'Do you think this teddy has a bead in its nose?' Peter shook his head. 'Shall we see?' Ben asked.

Quickly Laura took one of the beads from the bag on the trolley and slipped it into Ben's outstretched hand, along with a pair of dissecting forceps from the opened pack.

'I think we should have a look in his nose and see,' said Ben seriously.

Peter nodded.

Ben managed to grip the bead with the forceps without the child seeing him, and pretended to put the forceps into the bear's nose. 'See, he did have a bead,' Ben said, dropping the bead on to the palm of his hand.

Peter's eyes rounded. 'Ooh,' he said.

'Now I think we should look in your nose.' Ben tipped Peter back across his knees and tickled him. Laura had the pencil torch ready, with the angled forceps. 'I'm just going to look in your nose like I did teddy's,' Ben told Peter with a smile.

Before Peter could object Ben had removed the bead, with Laura shining the torch. She produced a sweet—some were kept especially for children on the bottom of the trolley—and unwrapped it. The crackle of the shiny paper distracted Peter before he could cry and he reached for the soft chocolate. 'That's for a good boy,' she said.

They were all smiling, mainly from relief that the removal of the bead had been accomplished with the least distress to the child.

'How many children do you have, Doctor?' Nicola Mitchell asked Ben shyly.

'None at the moment,' he said with a smile.

Nicola looked surprised. 'You were so good with Peter that I thought you must have at least six.'

Ben glanced at Laura, who blushed. 'I hope to have that many one day when I get married,' he said quietly, but the smile was no longer in his eyes.

Laura was filled with admiration for the way Ben had handled Peter, and this softened her towards him. He was an excellent doctor and deserved better than her cutting him off without a hearing. She loved him, and perhaps, if she could persuade him that there was no reason for him to be jealous of Martin, they could resume their relationship.

She was appalled at her selfishness. If you loved someone, you talked to them. What had she done? Run away because she couldn't bear to think that David had shortened his life to save her pain. Not that she believed he had. No one could be that unselfish.

So, instead of looking at him coldly, she smiled in return. Seeing her smile, Ben relaxed.

Martin coughed and said, 'Peter should be all right now, Mrs Mitchell.'

'Thank you, Doctor,' she said, putting the little boy into his pushchair.

Ben held the curtain aside for her and they left the cubicle.

Martin left them too. Ben and Laura stood side by side.

'Laura. . .'

'Ben. . .'

They both spoke each other's names at the same time. The little incident made them laugh and the strain between them lessened.

'I'd like to talk to you,' Laura said. 'I'm off duty now.'

Ben took her arm, holding it tightly, afraid she would change her mind. 'Good. Come on, then.'

'I have to change,' she said, laughing.

'Well, I'm coming with you. I don't want you to escape.'

'I promise not to do that,' she said with a serious face.

She changed quickly, and together they left in his car.

CHAPTER TWELVE

BEN drove Laura to his home. They didn't speak on the way, but their awareness of each other spoke for them in the almost tangible tension between them.

Laura wanted to touch him so badly that she leant towards him, drawn by the strength of her desire, and she knew he was feeling the same by the reckless way he was driving. He skidded to a halt outside his house and left the car there in the road. He had her door open before she could turn the handle and was reaching for her hand.

She placed hers in his and found that it was trembling as she smiled up into his face.

Ben drew her to him and kissed her where they stood, unable to restrain himself any longer. It was Laura who gently pushed him away, though she wanted him as much as he wanted her. 'I think we'd better go in,' she said drily. 'Before the neighbours gather.'

Ben glanced about him and saw an elderly couple standing, watching with interest. He laughed, and, putting his arm around her waist, drew her into the house.

Once inside he took her hand, and was about to lead her up the stairs when she said, 'I think we should have our talk first.' She knew that if he made love to her now she would be past caring whether he had acted out of jealousy or not.

Ben sighed as he released her. 'I suppose we must?' Laura nodded. 'I'll make us some coffee, or would you like something to eat?' he asked.

She felt food would have choked her and said, 'Coffee will be fine.'

She went with him into the kitchen and loved it as soon as she stepped over the threshold. It had been refurbished since she was a child. The units were good quality cream with a light oak edging, the floor covered in terracotta tiles. The walls were half covered in beige tiles, the other half with a paper that had matching curtains. The kitchen was large enough to hold a table and chairs.

Ben pulled out a chair for her to sit on and then filled the electric kettle. Laura found comfort in the small things that were to be found in most kitchens: toaster, kettle, calendar to write reminders on, and plants. A bunch of roses stood on the table in a glass vase.

'Mrs Taylor, the lady who cleans for me, picked those,' Ben explained as he took two mugs from one of the cupboards. 'Ordinary, or decaffeinated?' he asked.

'Ordinary, please.'

Laura watched his hands as he put the coffee into the cups and poured the water on to it. Every movement was co-ordinated. There was no dithering, no measuring the amount—a little more, a little less. In it went and the coffee was made. He made love the same way—smoothly, competently—the only difference was the passion that inspired his lovemaking.

Laura blushed at the thought of his hands moving

over her body, rousing her to unimaginable delights. Her hand trembled as she took the mug from him and a little of the liquid spilt on the table-top.

Ben pulled a piece of paper towel from the roller and wiped it away.

They drank their coffee in a silence that was full of sexual tension. 'Are you sure you want to talk now?' he asked, his voice husky with desire.

'Yes,' she whispered. 'I want everything to be straight between us before we make love.'

She finished her coffee and put the mug down. The noise it made as it touched the table seemed louder to her stretched nerves than it probably was.

'I want to assure you that you have no cause to be jealous. Martin is just a friend. In fact, he seems to be interested in Bea.' She watched his face carefully, to see if this piece of information disturbed him. Ben had been taking Bea around, after all.

'Good,' he said, relieved that Bea had not read more into their occasional outings.

'So there was no reason for you to tell that lie about David.' Laura held herself stiffly, afraid of what he would say next.

Ben saw how troubled she was. He also saw that she would not believe him if he repeated the truth he had told her at the ball. He wanted Laura, and loved her intensely. He didn't want to kill that love, so he lied. 'Can you forgive me for being so heartless?'

He looked so contrite that Laura rushed from the table to his side and flung her arms about him. 'Of course I forgive you,' she said, smiling down at him, her face relaxed and happy.

'That's all I wanted to know,' he said, smiling up into her face. Rising, Ben took her into his arms and wrapped her in a warm, protective embrace. 'Let's go to bed.'

They went upstairs, with his arm still about her.

Ben's lovemaking was gentle and considerate, almost like David's, Laura suddenly thought, unable to give herself fully. It was as if Ben was. . . What? Surely not sorry for her?

She felt frustrated, especially as she was sure his passion had been as urgent as her own. But the touch of his hand upon her sensitive skin lifted her to that exquisite peak, only to reach it before him. 'I'm sorry,' Ben said, kissing her gently, not on the lips but on the forehead. 'I've had a frustrating day.'

'That's all right, darling,' she whispered against his cheek.

But she felt he had held back, not like David had used to, in case he hurt her, but for some other reason, and this disturbed her greatly.

Laura snuggled against him and felt his arms tighten. Perhaps he would make love to her again. She was ready and eager, but he turned her so that she was cuddled with her back towards him and within seconds he was asleep. Perhaps it was just tiredness, she decided.

He woke her at eight o'clock with a cup of tea. 'Would you like to go out for a meal?' he asked.

He was dressed in a black short-sleeved shirt and black jeans. His hair was wet from the shower and curled at the nape. He looked big, powerful and sexy and she loved him, wanted him, now, this minute, but there was no corresponding desire in his eyes.

It had been a dull day, but the sunlight now shone palely through the window to touch one side of his face, leaving the other side in shadow.

The side she saw was smiling, but she had the uncanny feeling that the darkened side was serious. She was imagining it, she knew, and supposed she was thinking like this because of their unsatisfactory lovemaking.

'I think it would be nice if we ate here,' she said, hiding the disappointment he might see in her eyes by lowering them to take the cup from him.

A slight frown drew his eyebrows together. 'I don't think I have anything in the house that would make a meal.'

Was he making an excuse? Didn't he want her to stay?

'Wait a minute, though.' Ben had seen the doubt in her eyes and knew the reason for it, but he hadn't been able to help himself. The knowledge that he had told the truth about David had lain between them when they made love. 'There are eggs and salad. I could make an omelette.'

He smiled, as he thought cheerfully, but Laura saw a stiffness in his smile.

'I've had a shower,' Ben said. 'I've left dry towels, and here's a robe for you.' He pointed to a white towelling robe on the end of the bed.

'Thanks,' she said, reaching for the robe, suddenly shy with her naked body, something she had not been the first time they had made love.

Laura stayed longer in the shower than she would

normally have done. Somehow she dreaded going downstairs. She was distressed. Something was missing from their relationship.

As she towelled herself dry she decided that it was just their recent discord that was the cause and that they would settle back into their loving relationship given time.

Satisfied with this thought, she slipped on her jeans and navy blue sweatshirt, smiling at the penguin motif, then ran down the stairs.

Ben was beating the eggs. 'Can I do anything to help?' she asked.

'No, thanks,' he said, without looking up from his task. 'I've set the table and made the salad.'

'What about the bread?'

'Oh, yes.'

He smiled at her and she was relieved to see it was a genuine smile, without a hint of stiffness. Everything's going to be all right, she told herself, feeling her body relax.

Ben put down the bowl and lit the gas under the omelette pan. 'The bread's over there.' He gestured to the bread-bin on the dresser.

As Laura put pieces of brown bread on to the plates already on the table, she heard the sizzle of fat as Ben poured some of the egg into the frying-pan.

In a minute, he was handing her the omelette. 'Eat it while it's hot,' he told her. 'And help yourself to wine.'

She was already halfway through her omelette when he sat down in front of her. 'Can I pour you some wine?' she asked.

'Thanks.' He pushed the glass towards her.

They ate in silence, but it was a companionable silence. 'Mmm, that was good,' Laura said as she placed her knife and fork side by side on the empty plate. 'I can recommend your cooking!'

'Thanks.' He grinned across at her. 'But when we're married, I expect you to do all the cooking.'

'Oh, really?' she exclaimed. 'Don't you believe in equality of the sexes?'

'Absolutely not,' he said, trying to keep his face straight.

'Tough,' she said with a smile. 'You'll just have to get used to it.'

He left his seat and stretched out his hand. Laura took it and rose to stand in front of him. 'There's a lot we'll have to get used to, but we'll have plenty of time.' He took her face in his hands and kissed her gently, just the way David used to.

Laura trembled, not with desire, but with fear, because she felt that she had lost something precious and didn't know why.

Ben, seeing the troubled expression and the query in her eyes, was filled with a protective love, and kissed her again just as gently.

Laura could have cried. Where was her passionate lover? Much as she wanted to stay in his arms, she pushed him away. 'What's wrong?' she asked, trying, unsuccessfully, to hide her distress.

'Nothing, darling,' he said, moving to pull her towards him again.

Laura was not reassured. The expression on his face was loving, but it could have been David looking at her. She pulled away again. 'You don't have to treat me like porcelain.'

'I wasn't aware I was,' he said stiffly, trying to control his anger. Their unsatisfactory lovemaking, coupled with his letting her assume he had told her about David because he was jealous, was stretching his nerves.

She was losing him. Laura couldn't bear that. 'I'm sorry,' she said, throwing her arms around his neck and kissing him. 'I'm sorry, I'm sorry, I'm sorry.'

Ben's arms went round her in a tight embrace and his lips came down upon hers in a passionate kiss. What did it matter if he had lost a bit of his integrity, as long as his dearest love was happy?

Laura responded with an eagerness that was wanton. Her arms tightened, her kisses deepened. She entwined herself around him, desperate to hold him, love him, be part of him.

Ben swept her up into his arms and took her to the bedroom. Within seconds their clothes lay on the floor and they were making love with the frantic haste that their roused passions demanded. There was no gentle leading up to their final fulfilment. It happened rapidly, but ecstatically, and afterwards Ben looked down upon the face of a satisfied woman, whose eyes gazed langourously into his. The promise that had been in his kiss after they'd left the car had been fulfilled.

'I love you,' he said, his voice deepening with emotion.

Laura reached up and pulled his face down to hers. She kissed his eyelids and then his mouth, her lips trembling with the force of her love. 'And I love you, man of my heart.'

She stayed with him that night, fearful to leave in case she should lose him again, for she was sure she almost had.

As they sat at breakfast next morning, Ben said, 'I think we should get a special licence and get married as soon as possible.

'This time I admit you're right,' she said, grinning.

'Less of the cheek,' he admonished jokingly. 'Or I won't take you to get an engagement ring today.'

'I don't care whether I have an engagement ring or not, as long as I have you,' she said softly.

'We'll never get to work if you say things like that,' he told her, his eyes full of love.

This is what it will be like when we're married, thought Laura, as she took her place in the passenger seat of his car.

'I'll drop you at the corner,' Ben said as they neared the hospital. 'I don't want people looking snidely at you.'

'I don't care how they look,' she told him, but she appreciated his thoughtfulness.

Laura was about to step from the car when she saw a couple of schoolboys larking about, hitting each other with school-bags on the opposite pavement. She stopped with her hand on the door handle, held by a premonition.

'What is it?' Ben asked, thinking she had been suddenly taken unwell as her face had paled.

'Those boys. . .' Laura pointed.

Ben looked in the direction of her finger, and as

he did so saw one of the boys lose his balance and fall into the road in front of a car, which, fortunately, was slowing for the approaching corner.

They were both out of the car at the same time. A quick look up and down the road to make sure it was clear and they were across, kneeling beside the boy.

'I'm a doctor,' Ben said to reassure the boy, who was pale with shock, but not unconscious. 'Where does it hurt?'

At least he's not concussed, thought Laura, as the boy said in a faint whisper, 'It's my leg.' He tried to sit up, but fell back with a groan.

'Lie still,' Ben said. 'I'll just have a look at the rest of you.'

'What's your name?' Laura asked, with a reassuring smile.

'Jason Brown,' his friend told them, looking equally shocked. 'He's twelve.'

'Well, Jason Brown,' Ben said, after feeling the boy's limbs and looking into his eyes with the pencil torch which he always carried. 'It appears you have broken your leg, but nothing else seems to be damaged.'

A crowd of people going to offices and other work-places had gathered. The driver of the car was sitting on the pavement, looking shocked. 'He just fell in front of the car.' He sounded as if he could not believe it.

'I think you should come to the hospital for a rest,' Laura said, not liking the greyness of his face. He was a man of about fifty.

He looked up at her with dazed eyes. 'I must get to the office.'

'Perhaps a bit later, when you've recovered from the shock.'

'Perhaps you're right. I did have a heart by-pass operation two years ago.'

Ben had a car phone. He rang for an ambulance and it came within minutes, with the police. The driver was too shocked to explain what had happened and needed oxygen from one of the paramedics.

Laura told the police as much as she had seen, and this was confirmed by those in the crowd who had witnessed the accident. The boy who had been with Jason had fled the scene.

'We'll see you in Casualty in a few minutes,' Ben told Jason, leaving the paramedics to tend to him.

Laura went in the ambulance and Ben was waiting when the doors were opened. She had discovered that the driver's name was Phillip Tulley. He was looking much better now, and the oxygen mask was removed.

Jason's shock had subsided sufficiently for him to be taken straight to X-ray after Laura had taken his mother's name and address.

'I think you had better be admitted for a couple of days, Mr Tulley,' Ben said as the man was put into a wheelchair.

'All right,' Phillip said, looking less anxious.

Laura was rather surprised at the eagerness in Mr Tulley's tone. Usually patients couldn't wait to leave the hospital.

'We'll put you in a cubicle while I speak to the casualty registrar,' Ben said. 'Staff will admit you.'

Laura went to collect the necessary papers from Reception. 'I'll do it for you,' offered Karen Fletcher, one of the receptionists.

'Thanks, but it's no bother,' Laura told her as she collected the admission forms.

Phillip Tulley's colour had improved immensely by the time Laura returned. 'I'd much rather go home, but it would be better for my wife if I stayed here,' he said, after Laura had taken his details. 'She's just recovering from a hysterectomy.'

So that was the reason for his eagerness to stay, thought Laura. How considerate he was.

Suddenly she wondered if she had been as considerate with David. Had she thought of him before herself? Had she been unselfish? Searching her heart, Laura knew she had nothing to reproach herself with. She had devoted herself to him entirely.

She pushed these tormented thoughts to the bottom of her mind. They had suddenly reminded her of Ben's lying about David refusing chemotherapy. It had been a lie, hadn't it?

On the way to the medical ward she said, 'I'll phone your wife.' Concentrating on her patient was the way to quell her doubts.

'Thanks, Staff,' he said, looking more relaxed now he was in bed.

Laura mentioned to the staff nurse in charge of the ward that she had promised to contact Mr Tulley's wife.

'Oh, good,' Staff Nurse Howard said. 'One job less. We're short-staffed this morning.'

Laura was still in her plain clothes. She went to change, then joined Sister in the Casualty office. 'What's this I hear about you and Mr Kendricks arriving at the hospital together?' Sister Jackson gave Laura an arch look.

Laura had an insane desire to say, We came together because we slept together, but said instead, 'We arrived at the accident at the same time.' Which was not a lie, although not quite the truth.

'Ahhh?' Sister's raised eyebrows told Laura that Celia did not believe her.

'I told Mr Tulley that I would contact his wife for him,' Laura said hurriedly to distract Celia.

'Right. You can use this phone.'

Laura made the call. Mrs Tulley was grateful and promised to bring in her husband's pyjamas.

The rest of the day was spent in tending minor cases, many of which could have been treated by the patients' general practitioners. Stitches in cuts, sprained limbs, infected fingers, children's grazed knees.

Ben appeared when Laura was due to go off duty. 'How's the boy?'

'He had his fracture reduced and is in the children's ward.' Just to see Ben made her smile. 'His friend, the one who ran off, told his parents what had happened.'

'Just goes to show,' Ben said, putting an arm across her shoulders. 'You can never judge people.'

Like I did you? she thought. But I had good reason for doing so, hadn't I?

Feeling her tense under his arm, Ben realised how

stupid he had been. To distract her, he said, 'Sally's wedding is nearly here. I just wish it was ours.'

Laura glanced up into his face. 'So do I,' she said, with such a look of love that Ben drew her out of the patients' view, put his arms round her and kissed her.

Sister came out of the office just then, rounded the corner, and saw the registrar's arm around her staff nurse. 'I think you can go off duty now, Staff,' she said, her eyes twinkling.

'Thank you, Sister.' Laura grinned.

'Your place or mine?' Ben asked as they reached the car park.

'I have to go to Sally's for a fitting for my bridesmaid's dress,' Laura said, regret in her voice.

'What about later?' he asked as they took their seats in his car.

'Can't. It's her hen-night.'

'Oh, well.' Ben started the car. 'Come after that.'

The unsettled thoughts about David were still with her. She would have to sort those out. 'I think it would be better if I go home after,' she said, hoping he wouldn't feel hurt.

'Good idea.' He flashed a grin at her. 'Otherwise we would have another disturbed night.'

Laura laughed. They had reached her flat. Ben turned off the engine and, reaching for her, kissed her firmly, leaving her wishing she had agreed to go to his place later after all.

CHAPTER THIRTEEN

THE sun shone for Sally's wedding. They had decided to marry in a register office. Sally wore a short cream lace dress with short sleeves, the straight skirt fitted and slimming to her rather full figure. A pillar-box hat with a small veil and a posy of cream roses completed her outfit. Her cheeks were rosy with happiness and excitement.

Laura wore pink. Her dress was short, with a full skirt that showed off her slender legs to perfection. A pillar-box hat of the same material and a small posy of pink flowers completed her outfit.

Ben's eyes gleamed with appreciation when he saw her.

There were few guests, mainly friends of the couple. After the ceremony, the wedding breakfast was held in the park Pavilion, bringing back memories to Laura of that other time when she had dined there with Ben.

It was a happy occasion, enjoyed by all. After the meal, and after Laura and Ben had circulated, she asked him how Tracy Warren was.

'Fine. She was transferred to the psychiatric ward and Addison says she's responding well to treatment.'

'That's great.'

'What happened to Mr Tulley and that boy with the broken leg?' Ben asked.

'Mr Tulley went home after a week's rest and is keeping well. Jason had his leg plastered, then went home.'

'It's wonderful to hear of successes,' Ben said. 'I think they outweigh the failures, don't you?'

Laura considered his remark for a moment, then said, 'Yes. You're right.'

'It would be a shame to waste that dress,' Ben whispered in Laura's ear. 'How about my taking you dancing?'

'That would be marvellous,' Laura agreed. 'It's always a bit of a let-down after the happy couple leave.'

'My thoughts entirely.'

He drove her to his home and changed into evening dress. When he came back into the lounge, Laura's heart leapt into her mouth. He was the most attractive man she had ever seen.

Seeing the look in her eyes, Ben took her hand and raised her to her feet. 'Perhaps we should just dine here,' he whispered, close to her cheek.

Laura was breathless with desire.

'Do I take it you agree?' His eyes were dark with passion.

A soft sigh escaped her lips.

Ben swept her into his arms and carried her up the stairs. Gently he undressed her and she, with trembling fingers, struggled with the buttons of his dress-shirt.

Their lovemaking was passionate, but, for Laura, a certain frantic desperation drove her. She wanted to hold on to this man, never let him go. She was filled with a sudden fear that something would snatch

him from her. Was it the feeling that he was treating
her with too much consideration that made her think
this way? Even though she knew he was filled with a
desire to equal her own, she sensed that he was
holding back, and strove to break through this by
every touch, every kiss, every caress.

She thought she had succeeded when they reached
the height of their passion together, but as she lay in
his arms she felt a certain stiffness in the arm he had
about her.

They ate their meal in their dressing-gowns. It was
not a gourmet repast, just a cold meal he'd had in
the fridge, rolls and a bottle of wine.

'So, when are you going to marry me?' Ben asked,
wiping his mouth with a napkin.

Laura searched his eyes for signs of doubt, but
saw only love for her shining there. Reassured, she
said, 'As soon as possible,' with a smile.

'What about your parents?' Ben asked. 'You'll
want them to be here?'

'I suppose so,' Laura said, adding wistfully,
'Couldn't we just run away to Gretna Green?'
Laura's wedding to David had been a big affair. She
didn't want that again.

'If you want just the two of us we can have a
register office wedding,' he said evenly.

'The reason for marrying seems to be lost in the
build-up to a wedding and the crush of guests.' She
reached forward and took his hand. 'I want just us
and, if possible, a minister to marry us in a small
church.'

Ben's hand tightened on hers. 'I'm sure we'll be
able to find just such a place.'

He looked so positive that Laura asked, 'Where? How?'

'I happen to have an uncle who has just such a church.' He mentioned a parish close to Ledborough.

'But would he. . .?'

'He would,' Ben assured her. 'He believes as you do, and would respect our wishes.'

Laura left her seat and rushed to throw her arms around Ben's neck. He pulled her on to his knees and said, 'If you keep tempting me like this I'll be too exhausted to marry you.'

She laughed and continued to kiss him, so that he swept her up into his arms and into his bed.

Sunday morning they spent lazily making plans, and in the afternoon, after Laura had changed in her flat, they went to see Ben's uncle. He was delighted to agree to marry them and a date was fixed for September the twenty-seventh, just a month away.

On the way back in the car, Ben said, 'We'll tell the relatives after we're married. We can have a party for them then, but our day will be just for the two of us.'

He dropped her at the flat. 'See you tomorrow,' he promised.

Laura was on the late shift on Monday. It was a busy day, filled with attending to minor cuts and sprains. A patient with a deep laceration of the arm, caused when a shelf at the local pottery factory had fallen, sending broken pieces ricocheting about, was to go straight to Theatre. The cut, involving muscle, was too deep to stitch in Casualty.

Laura took the patient to Theatre, holding the damaged arm up to control the bleeding. An infusion was already in place to counteract shock.

She had hoped to see Ben in the canteen, but he was even busier than she was, according to Martin. 'An inpatient with an abdominal wound fell and burst his stitches,' he explained. 'So Ben's in Theatre.'

The night staff came on at quarter to ten. Laura and Susan Hadley attended to the patients while Sister handed over to the night staff.

There was only one patient waiting to be seen when two youths burst into Casualty. One had a cut head, with blood trickling down his face.

Laura tensed as soon as she saw them. Past experience had warned her that they might be trouble. The police had had to be called in on some such occasions.

But these lads appeared quiet. 'Someone hit Harry on the head with a bottle,' the uninjured one told her.

Laura took Harry to a cubicle with his friend following. 'You wait here.' She gestured to the seats in the waiting area. 'You can see your friend when he's been stitched. Phone for Martin, please, Susan,' she instructed the nurse as Harry's friend left the cubicle.

'Sister sent me to take over from you,' said Winifred Baxter, who was on night duty now, as she parted the cubicle curtains.

'Thanks.' It was not often that the day staff could leave on time.

Laura couldn't rid herself of a feeling of disquiet as she left.

Perhaps it was the insolent way Harry had looked at her, she decided as she settled her shoulder-bag in place. She had been treated like that before, but this time he had seemed to be laughing at her as well.

Martin passed her with a cheery 'Goodnight' as she headed for the exit.

As she passed through the waiting area Laura noticed that Harry's friend was not seated there. Perhaps he had gone for drink of tea. There was a coffee- and tea-machine quite near to the resuscitation-room.

She glanced in its direction, but did not see him. Shrugging, she was about to turn away, when she heard a noise coming from the resuscitation-room.

Hurrying forward, she flung the door open. Harry's friend was stuffing syringes, needles and any ampoules he could find into a bag he had produced from his pocket.

'I thought something was wrong,' she said, walking towards him. 'Did you cause his cut?'

The youth's face became ugly. 'You're too clever by half,' he said, making a grab for her.

Laura's bag fell from her shoulder, the loose clasp—which she had meant to have repaired—burst open and the hairspray she had bought from the hospital shop at lunchtime rolled out. Her assailant grabbed it, flipped the top off and squirted it in her face.

Her hands flew to her burning eyes, but she managed to put a foot out as he rushed past, causing them both to fall heavily through the door into the passage at Ben's feet.

Laura didn't know what was happening to her assailant and did not care. She only knew that her eyes were paining her intensely.

She heard scuffling, and then Ben's voice beside her ear saying, 'Don't touch your eyes, sweetheart.'

She supposed it must have been his arms that scooped her up so gently and laid her down on the resuscitation trolley.

'I'll instil some amethocaine eye-drops to ease the pain, Sister, then she'll need saline wash-outs,' he said.

'Don't touch my eyes,' Laura begged, raising her hands to ward him off.

'I only want to ease your pain,' Ben told her gently. 'You know the amethocaine will do that, and then we can wash your eyes out with saline.'

Laura had treated eyes before and knew he was telling her the truth. 'I'm sorry,' she murmured. 'I'll try and co-operate.'

'There's my brave girl,' Ben said, and she could hear the catch in his voice. 'Hold her hands, please, Sister,' he instructed Linda Connelly.

Laura wanted to scratch her eyes out with the pain, and knew this was why Ben had asked Linda to help him. 'Martin. . .' she heard Ben say. So Martin was there too. Of course. Ben would need the two of them to instil the drops.

She tried not to cry out, and felt pleased when

Ben said, 'That's my good girl,' after he had instilled the drops.

Laura felt him take her shaking hands from Linda. She knew they were his hands because they were big and strong, yet gentle. 'You'll feel better shortly, my darling,' he said. And she did, as soon as the anaesthetising drops acted. 'We'll have to wash your eyes out with saline and then you'll have them covered for a while.' He felt her hands clench in his. 'Don't be afraid,' he told her gently. 'I'll be with you all the time.'

'Thank you,' she whispered, wishing she could see his dear face.

She flickered her lids to do so, but he said, 'Don't try and open your eyes. Let them rest.'

Laura was taken to a side-ward attached to Female Medical. She didn't feel her eyes being washed out because of the local anaesthetic, but when that began to wear off her eyes were not as painful and she was grateful for this.

She knew that Ben was doing her treatment, for she heard him tell the night staff that they could leave Laura to him. How kind he was. Not only to herself, but to the night staff. Another person would have left the treatment to the nurses.

Laura didn't know what the time was, but as her eyes felt less painful she said, 'Do go home and get some sleep, Ben, dear.'

'Trying to get rid of me?' he joked.

She stretched out her hand and felt it taken in his warm one. 'Never that,' she whispered.

She felt a kiss, which was just a whisper on her forehead, and sighed. 'You're so good to me,' she said, feeling tears not due to the spray well in her eyes, soaking the pads.

Ben removed the damp pads and replaced them with dry ones. 'I can sleep during the day,' he said.

How comforting his presence was. As she lay awake she eventually heard his even breathing and knew that he was sleeping. Suddenly she realised just what a wonderful man he was. Ben had told her the truth about David, but when he had seen how she could not accept it he had pretended that it was jealousy that had made him tell her. He had done it out of love for her, just as David had.

Laura knew that in the morning the ophthalmic specialist would examine her eyes, and staining would be instilled to see if any damage had occurred. What if I should be blind? she thought, panicking.

Suddenly she knew with a certainty that must have been equal to her dead husband's that she would not want Ben to be tied to her if this was so. She loved him enough to give him up, rather than have him suffer, watching her struggle. It was just as hard on the loved one, if not more so, as it was on the victim.

At last she understood why David had sacrificed what remained of his life. It wasn't easy to accept, and she would always feel guilty, but she knew now why he had done it.

She must tell Ben. But she would wait until the specialist had been tomorrow.

CHAPTER FOURTEEN

LAURA knew that Ben was not in the room when she awoke. She knew because she could not feel his presence. A feeling of desolation far worse than that which had swept over her at David's death threatened to overwhelm her.

This is what it will be like if I find I'm blind and give him up, she told herself. The love she felt for Ben was more than desire, it warmed every part of her being. It made her feel alive, vital, whole. If she gave him up she would be lost, but if she was blind it had to be done.

It must be daylight, she thought, for it was not as dark behind her pads as it had been during the night. Surely that must be a good sign?

She longed to snatch the pads away, to see if her sight was whole, but fear that she was blind held her back.

Ben had reassured her during the night. 'I'm sure your eyes will be fine,' he had said, sensing her unspoken fear.

His confidence had uplifted her, but now that he was not here her fears returned afresh to torment her. Laura heard the door open and raised her hand. It was taken in a firm grasp—Ben's grasp. 'Did you get a fright to find me not here?' he asked. 'I just went for a wash.'

'No,' Laura lied. 'I've just woken.'

'The tablets we gave you helped you to sleep?' he asked.

Laura could hear the loving concern in his voice and said, 'Yes,' though she had slept little.

The door opened again. 'Nurse has come to give you a wash,' Ben told her. 'Alan Watson will be coming early, so you won't have long to wait.' Alan Watson was the ophthalmic consultant. 'I'll leave you to Nurse's tender care,' he said, releasing her hand.

'You'll come back?' Laura could not stop herself from asking. How weak I am, she chastised herself. She had decided, when she had woken and found herself alone, that it would be better to see the consultant without Ben being present. She felt she could cope better with bad news if he was not there. Now here she was, almost begging him to stay.

Warm lips touched hers gently. She smelt the tangy fragrance of the soap he used as he laid his cheek on hers for a moment. 'Of course I will. Wouldn't miss the unveiling for anything,' he joked, but Laura heard the strain in his voice.

She was washed and dressed in a pretty nightgown that the night nurse had lent her when Ben returned.

It seemed ages before Alan Watson came. All the time that Ben chatted and tried to keep her spirits up part of her was thinking how long the days must seem if you were blind. How dreadful not to be able to see the leaves turn from green to brown, the sky darken, the sea change colour, the expression on a loved one's face. She had never really thought about it before. How would she cope in a world of darkness? Would she be able to adjust?

Laura had not realised Ben had stopped talking, her mind was so occupied with her thoughts, until he said, 'Don't worry.'

'I'm not,' she answered cheerfully, tightening her hand in his. 'I was just thinking of how I would like to visit my parents in Canada.'

'We'll go together,' he said brightly. 'Make it a honeymoon trip to America as well.'

Laura detected concern in his tone. Had he read her thoughts? Did he know that she planned to leave him if she was blind?

She heard the door open and knew it must be the consultant. 'Well, well,' Alan Watson said in his bluff way. He was more like an army officer than a doctor, but everybody knew his bluff manner concealed a kind heart. 'We'll just have a look at your eyes now,' he said. 'Close the curtains, please, Sister.'

His fingers were so gentle that Laura did not feel the pads being removed. It was the breath of air on her lids that told her so. 'I'm just going to bathe your eyelids, then I want you to open your eyes,' he told her.

After her eyelids were dried, she was frightened to open them.

'Don't be afraid,' he said kindly.

Laura opened her eyes slowly. She could see— hazily—she could see his face smiling down at her. 'I can see,' she whispered, tears stinging her eyes.

'Good,' he said. 'But we'll need to put some staining in to check your eyes are all right.'

Laura turned her head to search for Ben. She saw

the tears of relief in his eyes and knew he had been as anxious as she.

Gently Alan dried her eyes and put in the staining. She didn't care that it stung. She could bear anything now. He looked carefully into each eye with the ophthalmoscope. 'Fine. Everything's fine,' he told her. 'Your eyes will be sore for a bit, but we'll give you some drops for that, and the redness on your skin will fade.'

'Oh, thank you,' she said, tears gathering again.

'It's always a pleasure to give good news,' Alan said, smiling.

Laura wondered how often he had to give bad news.

'I think you should wear dark glasses for a while,' Alan told her. 'Is there someone at home to look after you?'

'Yes,' said Ben.

'Ahh? Do I detect a romance?' Alan asked jovially.

'Indeed, you do. Laura is to be my wife.'

'Congratulations.' Alan shook their hands, chatted for a minute or two, then left.

Ben sat on the bed and took Laura's hands in his. 'Well, darling.' The lines of strain were still noticeable upon his face. 'I think you should have a short rest, then dress and come home with me.'

Home with Ben. How wonderful that sounded. 'Ben,' she whispered, but the words to tell him that she knew he had told her the truth about David were held back by a swell of emotion so great she could not speak. She could marry Ben now. All the torment of the night lay in stressful lines upon her face. It looked pinched, older.

Tears pricked in Ben's eyes. How he loved this girl. Her pain had been his pain, her fear had been his fear, and the thought that she would refuse to marry him if she had been found to be blind still lingered hauntingly in his mind. He knew what she had been thinking, though not that she had paralleled herself with David.

He suppressed the desire that heated his skin, but could not stop himself from taking her gently into his arms and kissing her lips.

A passion so strong rose within Laura, as she kissed him back and put her arms about him tightly, that she would have pulled him down on the bed.

'Hey!' he said, drawing back with a laugh. 'That's not fair, taking advantage of a helpless male like this.

'It must be the bed,' Laura said, grinning. 'Its use for other things. . .' Her implication was clear.

'So it's my body you're after,' he said, his arms tightening about her.

'Absolutely,' she whispered against his cheek.

Ben had to use great self-control to stop himself from making love to her, there and then. She was as desperate as he was to relieve the strain they had both been suffering, to reaffirm their love by touch of hand and lip, and the closeness of their bodies.

He put her from him and said, 'I think you should forgo your rest, get dressed and come home with me now, don't you?' There was a mischievous twinkle in his eyes.

'I'll endorse that.' Laura smiled at him.

It didn't take long for her to dress. Sister gave her some eyedrops and told her to wear dark glasses for the next couple of days. 'Dr Watson wants to see you at his clinic next week.' She gave Laura an outpatient card with the day and time.

Laura thanked them all for their kindness as she stood with Ben's hand under her elbow. She could feel his impatience and was tempted to tease him by prolonging her goodbyes, but the touch of his hand on her elbow roused a desire to feel more than just a touch, so she said goodbye and they left.

The sun was shining as she stepped from the hospital, and she paused to allow it to caress her face.

On the way to his house, Laura looked at the buildings, the road, the trees, the sky, as if she was seeing them for the first time. I will try never to take my sight for granted again, she promised.

When they arrived at Rosemary Gardens Ben stopped the car outside his house and opened the passenger door for her. He paused on the step and handed her the key. 'You're home,' he said. 'I've bought it.'

He was rewarded by the joy he saw in her face and by the kiss she gave him. This house was theirs. Ben took her hand and led her inside. 'How lucky I am,' she whispered as he closed the door behind them.

He took her into his arms and said, 'I'm the lucky one.'

There was such love in his eyes that Laura took off her glasses and, putting her arms round his neck, kissed him, hoping that this would show him how much she felt, how much she loved him.

'My love,' he whispered.

They climbed the stairs together. Their previous urgency had left them. In its place was a feeling of deep contentment.

She glanced up into Ben's eyes as they stood facing each other in the bedroom, and detected a touch of sadness there. Immediately she understood why.

Gently she pulled him down to sit beside her on the bed. 'Ben, darling, I have a confession to make.'

'You're pregnant?' His eyes lit with delight. They hadn't used a contraceptive.

'No.' She smiled, then her face became serious. 'I've admitted to myself that you were telling me the truth about David.' Tears smarted in her eyes.

The last barrier had gone. 'Oh, my darling. Don't cry. David would have wanted you to live a full life.' He kissed her gently on the lips. 'I did try to persuade him to have the treatment,' Ben said earnestly. 'I told him how my mother had had terminal cancer, and how the three years' remission she gained by having chemotherapy brought us, as a family, closer together.'

He paused for a moment and Laura, looking into his eyes, saw not the sadness she would have expected to see, but a calmness. He took a deep breath. 'My father and I had always been at logger-heads, but my mother's illness drew the best out of us and her last years were the happiest I have ever known until this moment.' He smiled down at her lovingly.

'That's one of the nicest compliments I have ever had,' she said, hugging him. 'But chemotherapy works wonders with many cancers, doesn't it?' she asked.

'Oh, yes. It was just that both my mother's and David's cancers were inoperable, and too far advanced.'

They remained silent for a little while, until the sadness of losing their loved ones subsided.

Laura lifted her face to his and Ben kissed her eyes, her cheeks, and enfolded her in his warm, strong arms. Then he undressed her and she undressed him. Lying together, they drew comfort from making gentle love and found a new strength in their coming together.

The rest of the day was spent in just simple things: eating, laughing, watching the television.

But that night they made love passionately, banishing the anguish they had felt, with every touch, every kiss, committing themselves to each other until the peak they reached together was a communion of their souls.

The guilt they had felt at being attracted to each other while David was alive, and the discord this and Laura's belief that Ben was responsible for her husband not having chemotherapy had brought, were swept away like winter leaves, preparing the ground for spring. The spring of their new life together.

As the morning light shone through the curtains they awoke, arms about each other. 'I love you, Laura,' Ben whispered, close to her face.

'And I you, my darling,' she said, with a catch in her voice.

'You do know this house has five bedrooms, don't you?' Ben asked, with a twinkle in his eye.

Laura looked up into his face. 'So?' She frowned.

'Well, it would be criminal not to fill them.'

'Fill them? How?' She looked at him with a puzzled frown.

'Children! You heard Peter's mother ask if I had any children.'

'Yes,' Laura almost shrieked. 'And I heard your reply.'

Ben nodded his head. 'Six.'

'Six?' Laura's mouth gaped.

'Yes.' He grinned. 'So we had better start right away.'

Laura laughed. 'Well, if you insist.' She raised her face for his kiss, and as his kiss deepened she revelled in her good fortune. To be loved by such a man was to be blessed.

MILLS & BOON

CHRISTMAS CRACKERS

A cracker of a gift pack full of
Mills & Boon goodies. You'll find...

Passion—in *A Savage Betrayal* by Lynne Graham

A beautiful baby—in *A Baby for Christmas* by Anne McAllister

A Yuletide wedding—in *Yuletide Bride* by Mary Lyons

A Christmas reunion—in *Christmas Angel* by Shannon Waverly

Special Christmas price of 4 books
for £5.99 (usual price £7.96)

Published: November 1995

Available from WH Smith, John Menzies, Volume One, Forbuoys, Martins,
Tesco, Asda, Safeway and other paperback stockists.

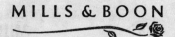

MILLS & BOON

Kids & Kisses—where kids and romance go hand in hand.

This winter Mills & Boon brings you Kids & Kisses— a set of titles featuring lovable kids as the stars of the show!

Look out for
The Secret Baby by Day Leclaire
Doctor Wentworth's Babies by Frances Crowne
in November 1995 (Love on Call series).

Kids…one of life's joys, one of life's treasures.

Kisses…of warmth, kisses of passion, kisses from mothers and kisses from lovers.

In Kids & Kisses…every story has it all.

Available from W.H. Smith, John Menzies, Forbuoys, Martins, Tesco, Asda, Safeway and other paperback stockists.

A years supply of Mills & Boon Romances — absolutely free!

Would you like to win a years supply of heartwarming and passionate romances? Well, you can and they're FREE! All you have to do is complete the wordsearch puzzle below and send it to us by 30th April 1996. The first 5 correct entries picked after that date will win a years supply of Mills & Boon Romance novels (six books every month — worth over £100). What could be easier?

STOCKHOLM	PARIS	HELSINKI	ANKARA
REYKJAVIK	LONDON	ROME	AMSTERDAM
COPENHAGEN	PRAGUE	VIENNA	OSLO
MADRID	ATHENS	LIMA	

N	O	L	S	O	P	A	R	I	S
E	Q	U	V	A	F	R	O	K	T
G	C	L	I	M	A	A	M	N	O
A	T	H	E	N	S	K	E	I	C
H	L	O	N	D	O	N	H	S	K
N	S	H	N	R	I	A	O	L	H
E	D	M	A	D	R	I	D	E	O
P	R	A	G	U	E	U	Y	H	L
O	A	M	S	T	E	R	D	A	M
C	R	E	Y	K	J	A	V	I	K

Please turn over for details on how to enter

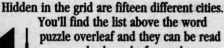

Hidden in the grid are fifteen different cities. You'll find the list above the word puzzle overleaf and they can be read backwards, forwards, up, down and diagonally. As you find each city, circle it or put a line through it.

When you have found all fifteen, don't forget to fill in your name and address in the space provided below and pop this page in an envelope (you don't need a stamp) and post it today. Hurry – competition ends 30th April 1996.

Mills & Boon Capital Wordsearch
FREEPOST
Croydon
Surrey
CR9 3WZ

Are you a Reader Service Subscriber?   Yes ☐   No ☐

Ms/Mrs/Miss/Mr _____

Address _____

_____

_____ Postcode _____